# IOWA

*Written by*
## Jenny Schwartz

*Music by*
## Todd Almond

*Lyrics by*
## Todd Almond & Jenny Schwartz

A SAMUEL FRENCH ACTING EDITION

**SAMUEL**
**FRENCH**
FOUNDED 1830

SAMUELFRENCH.COM
SAMUELFRENCH-LONDON.CO.UK

---

### FOR PRODUCTION ENQUIRIES

#### UNITED STATES AND CANADA
Info@SamuelFrench.com
1-866-598-8449

#### UNITED KINGDOM AND EUROPE
Plays@SamuelFrench-London.co.uk
020-7255-4302

Each title is subject to availability from Samuel French, depending upon country of performance. Please be aware that *IOWA* may not be licensed by Samuel French in your territory. Professional and amateur producers should contact the nearest Samuel French office or licensing partner to verify availability.

---

## MUSIC USE NOTE

*IOWA* was first produced by Playwrights Horizons at the Peter Jay Sharp Theater in New York City on March 20, 2015. The performance was directed by Ken Rus Schmoll, with sets by Dane Laffrey, costumes by Arnulfo Maldonado, lights by Tyler Micoleau, sound by Daniel Kluger, and music direction by J. Oconer Navarro. The Production Stage Manager was Richard A. Hodge. The cast was as follows:

**YOUNGER BECCA / CHILD** . . . . . . . . . . . . . . . . . . . . . . . . . Kolette Tetlow

**SANDY** . . . . . . . . . . . . . . . . . . . . . . . . . . . . . . . . . . . Karyn Quackenbush

**BECCA** . . . . . . . . . . . . . . . . . . . . . . . . . . . . . . . . . . . . . . . . . Jill Shackner

**ROGER / MR. HILL / JIM / PONY** . . . . . . . . . . . . . . . . . . . . . . Lee Sellars

**AMANDA / LATINA NANCY DREW / SISTER WIFE** . . . . . Amanda Sanchez

**BLACK NANCY DREW / SISTER WIFE** . . . . . . . . . . . . . . . . . . April Matthis

**LIZ / ASIAN NANCY DREW / TRANSGENDER NANCY DREW /**
**SISTER WIFE** . . . . . . . . . . . . . . . . . . . . . . . . . . . . . . . . . . . Cindy Cheung

**CHEERLEADER / JEWISH NANCY DREW / SISTER WIFE** . . . . . . . . . . Annie
McNamara

*IOWA* was developed at the 2013 Sundance Institute Theatre Lab at MASS MoCA.

*IOWA* was workshopped as part of the Frederick Loewe Award, a program of New Dramatists.

*IOWA* was developed with the generous participation of the Bats at The Flea Theater.

# CHARACTERS

**YOUNGER BECCA / CHILD** – female, 8ish

**SANDY** – female, 40s-50s

**BECCA** – female, teenager - can be played by young woman

**ROGER / MR. HILL / JIM / PONY** – female, 40s-50s

**AMANDA / LATINA NANCY DREW / SISTER WIFE** – female, 20s-40s

**BLACK NANCY DREW / SISTER WIFE** – female, 20s-40s

**LIZ / ASIAN NANCY DREW / TRANSGENDER NANCY DREW / SISTER WIFE** – female, 20s-40s

**CHEERLEADER / JEWISH NANCY DREW / SISTER WIFE** – female, 20s-40s

Various other characters to be played by the ensemble.

## MUSICAL NUMBERS

1. "How Many Miles Could It Really Be?" . . . **CHILD, COMPANY**
2. "Coastal Erosion" . . . . . . . . . . . . . . . . . . . . . . . . . . . **COMPANY**
3. "Jesus' Bones/Should I Be Worried?" . . . **LIZ, CHEERLEADER**
4. "Cheerleaders" . . . . . . . . . . . . . . . . . . . . . **AMANDA, COMPANY**
5. "This is America" . . . . . . . . . . **LIZ, AMANDA, CHEERLEADER, NANCY DREW**
6. "Ponies" . . . . . . . . . . . . . . . . . . . . . . . . . . . . . **ROGER (PONY)**
7. "Psst...I'm a Poet" . . . . . . . . . . . . . . . . . . . . . . . . . . . **BECCA**
8. "Fun!" . . . . . . . . . . . . . . . . . . . **SANDY, LIZ, CHILD, AMANDA, CHEERLEADER, NANCY DREW**
9. "I Don't Know" . . . . . . . . . . . . . . . . . . . . . . . . **SANDY, BECCA**
10. "Psst I'm Not a Poet" . . . . . . . . . . . . . **SISTER WIVES, BECCA**
11. "Oratorio" . . . . . . . . . . . . . . . . . . . . . . **SISTER WIVES, SANDY**
12. "Iowa" . . . . . . . . . . . . . . . . . . . . . . . . . . . . . . . . . . . . **COMPANY**
13. "I Am a Hawk" . . . . . . . . . . . . . . . . . . . . . . . . . . . . . **COMPANY**

*(A **CHILD** is alone onstage.)*

**[MUSIC NO. 1: "HOW MANY MILES?"]**

**CHILD.**
> HOW MANY MILES
> COULD IT REALLY BE?
> I'VE GOT A BIKE AND A PAIR OF SKATES.
> I'LL TAKE A BOOK
> AND A LAMP
> SO I CAN READ MYSELF TO SLEEP EACH NIGHT

> *(**COMPANY** enters.)*

**BECCA & LIZ.** OH…

| **CHILD.** | **BECCA & LIZ** |
|---|---|
| HOW MANY DAYS | HOW?… |
| COULD IT REALLY TAKE? | |

| **CHILD, BECCA, LIZ.** | **COMPANY.** |
|---|---|
| I SEE IT SO I KNOW | |
| I CAN GET THERE | |
| IT CAN'T BE MUCH | MMM… |
| FARTHER THAN | |
| DOWNTOWN OR PARIS | |
| OR THAT PLACE I GO IN | MM MMM… |
|   MY DREAMS | |

**COMPANY.**
> OH…
> PEOPLE SAY THEY'VE MEASURED THE DISTANCE
> AND THAT IT'S SO FAR
> SO FAR THAT YOU WOULD SPEND
> MORE THAN MOST OF YOUR LIFE
> JUST GETTING THERE

**CHILD, BECCA, LIZ.**
> BUT PEOPLE WILL TELL YOU ANYTHING

1

**CHILD.**

    NOT ON MARS
    NOT ON MARS
    NOT ON MARS

# PART I

## HOME

*(Lights up on* **SANDY***'s suburban home.)*

*(***SANDY*** is video chatting with* **ROGER***.)*

*(***ROGER***'s voice is heard through the computer.)*

*(***SANDY***'s daughter* **BECCA** *enters with her friend* **AMANDA***.)*

**BECCA.** Hi, Mom.

**SANDY.** Hello, girls.

**BECCA.** Can Amanda stay for dinner?

**SANDY.** I don't see why not.

**BECCA.** What's with the champagne?

**SANDY.** Funny you should ask.

I have some very exciting news.

Roger has asked me to marry him.

**BECCA.** Roger?

Who's Roger?

**SANDY.** My boyfriend, silly.

**ROGER.** *(correcting her)* Your fiancé.

**SANDY.** *(swooning)* My fiancé.

I like the sound of that.

**BECCA.** Wait a minute.

You mean your Facebook friend?

**SANDY.** My Facebook fiancé.

To be precise.

I've already changed my relationship status.

Roger walked me through it.

All you do is go to 'edit my profile' and then 'relationships' and then click on the arrow and scroll down to 'engaged' and *let go*!

Easy peasy lemon squeezy!

**ROGER.** Don't forget to save your changes.

**SANDY.** Jesus gave me a thumbs up sign.

**BECCA.** Jesus?

**SANDY.** Jesus the janitor.

The janitor at work.

I'm going to miss that guy.

**BECCA.** What do you mean miss him?

**SANDY.** I quit my job.

**BECCA.** You're kidding, right?

**SANDY.** Becca, do you have wax in your ears?

We are going to live with Roger.

Now, chin up, shoulders back, pull yourself together.

There's someone very special I've been wanting you to meet.

**ROGER.** Hi Becky.

**BECCA.** Becca.

**ROGER.** Hi Becca.

**BECCA.** Hi.

**ROGER.** First things first, I have no intention of replacing your –

**SANDY.** Excuse for a father?

Replace away!

**ROGER.** In that case, call me Dad.

**SANDY.** And this is Amanda.

Becca's only friend.

Don't mind Amanda.

Comes from a broken home.

Antisocial.

Prone to violence.

Eating disorder.

ADD.

You sure know how to pick 'em.

**ROGER.** LOL.

**SANDY.** OMG and FYI, OCD!

Show them the ring.

**ROGER.** Voila.

**SANDY.** A sapphire.

**ROGER.** Yep!

To match the blue in your eyes.

**BECCA.** Her eyes are green.

**ROGER.** Then, we'll switch it for an emerald.

**SANDY.** Bite your tongue.

The ring is perfection.

And so are you.

**ROGER.** I love you, Sandy.

**SANDY.** I love you, Roger.

**ROGER.** Cheers!

**SANDY.** To happy endings.

Wink wink.

Girls, would you excuse us?

We'd like a little privacy.

(*to* **BECCA**)

Have you ever heard of cyber sex?

It's similar to phone sex, except you use a computer!

**BECCA.** Mom, oh my God, we've heard of cyber sex, OK?

**SANDY.** Becca Jones, you're twelve years old, don't tell me you're a slut.

**BECCA.** I'm not a slut.

**SANDY.** Thank God.

**BECCA.** I'm also not twelve.

**SANDY.** How old are you?

**BECCA.** Fourteen.

**SANDY.** (*panic*) Heavens to Betsy, that makes me eighty-five.

**BECCA.** Forty-five.

**SANDY.** Impossible.

Seems like just yesterday I was a shy little zygote.

Slithering down the fallopian tube.

Isn't it amazing?

After all these years, I still miss slithering.

Ah, to be an embryo...

Without a care in the womb.

**ROGER.** You'll always be my spring chicken.

**SANDY.** Bock bock.

**ROGER.** Cluck cluck.

**SANDY.** Roger, do you slither?

**ROGER.** Like a snake.

**SANDY.** Cock of the walk!

Now, Becca, a word on the slut front.

Regarding sexuality, I believe in honesty and education.

Openness and information.

Have a seat.

I'd like to level with you.

Are you familiar with the birds and the bees?

**BECCA.** Uh huh.

**SANDY.** The stork?

**BECCA.** Yeah.

**SANDY.** *(surprised and relieved)* Great!

Any questions?

**BECCA.** I don't think so.

**SANDY.** Moving on.

In conclusion, do as I say not as I do.

Everything in moderation.

Your body is a temple and so on and so forth.

I'm *so* glad we had this little chat.

Regarding masturbation, it does not cause blindness.

As far as I can see.

Beware of ovulation.

Leads to bouts of menstruation.
Highly contagious.
Oftentimes fatal.
Welcome to womanhood.
Nasty nasty.

Have a Motrin.
Or three.
Consider yourself warned.
Steer clear of menopause.
And peri-menopause.
More soon.

I'm back.
Peri-menopause.
Colon.
The pits.
Insomnia.
Night sweats.
Exhaustion.
Mood swings.
Where's my old self?
Question mark.
Smiley face.
Post.

BTW.
Are you a lesbian?
Not to pry.
I only ask because men are slime.
With the exception of Jesus the janitor.
And what's his name?

**ROGER.** Roger.

**SANDY.** Knock wood.
Do you consider yourself femme or butch?
Or in between?
Not to label.

Labeling is disabling.

A child is not a soup can, and don't let anybody tell you different.

Roger, care to back me up here?

**ROGER.** Nasty nasty.

**SANDY.** You're turning me on.

*(to* **BECCA***)*

Champagne?

**BECCA.** I'll pass.

**SANDY.** On the flip side, nobody likes a goody-two-shoes.

This year's goody-two-shoes is next year's spinster.

**BECCA.** I'm not a goody-two-shoes.

**SANDY.** Becca, face facts.

Everyone calls you *Book*ah for a reason.

**BECCA.** Sorry, but no one's ever called me Bookah.

**SANDY.** Well, they should.

It's apt.

All work and no play.

Dull dull dull.

*(to* **ROGER***)*

She was basically born with a book up her nose.

**BECCA.** You mean my nose in a book?

**SANDY.** It's a wonder we're related.

What with me being the life of the party.

Let's dance!

Or better yet, slither.

Get a load of this.

Bookah writes poetry.

**BECCA.** How do you know?

**SANDY.** *(past tense)* I read your diary.

**BECCA.** *(past tense)* You read my diary?

**SANDY.** At least, I tried.

Wow, what a snoozer.

Put me straight to sleep.

**BECCA.** Where are you going?

**SANDY.** Back in a flash.

**BECCA.** Get out of my room.

**SANDY.** I have a few questions.

**BECCA.** Give me back my diary.

**SANDY.** Inside voice!

Wait your turn!

Hands and feet to yourself!

Language!

Now, first of all, who's Mr. Hill?

**BECCA.** Mr. Hill is my math teacher.

**SANDY.** Your math teacher's a lesbian?

**BECCA.** So what if he's forty and balding.

I'm in love.

*(**SANDY** snores. Just one loud snore.)*

Jesus.

**SANDY.** *(waking up)* Jesus the janitor?

Where?

**BECCA.** You fell asleep.

**SANDY.** Case and point.

Better than gin or Ambien.

Or melatonin.

Works like a charm.

Listen up, Missy.

One more poem out of you and you're grounded.

Live a little.

You know, I have a diary too, and it goes something like this:

Dear Diary.

Jesus loves me.

If only he wasn't a janitor, I'd jump his bones.

Dear Diary.

I jumped Jesus' bones.

**SANDY**. *(cont.)* Dear Diary.

Dear Jesus.

If only you weren't a janitor.

If only you didn't have herpes.

If only *I* didn't have herpes.

Jesus gave me *herpes.*

The thing is, I still love Jesus, even though I'm suffering.

Even though Jesus cheats on me.

With hookers.

Don't tell what's his name.

**ROGER**. Roger.

**BECCA**. Jesus gave you herpes?

**SANDY**. Have you been reading my diary?

You little snoop!

Go to your room!

Tweens.

**BECCA**. Mom, I'm not a tween.

**SANDY**. My bad.

Are you a toddler?

Are you a slutty toddler?

Now that's just wrong.

"How to talk to your tween about their celebrity idol."

"How to make your tween think you're cool.

Share a hobby."

Yoo hoo.

Just me.

Who's your celebrity idol?

Nancy Drew?

Elmo?

Cher?

As far as hobbies, I like spinning.

And tanning.

And being tan.

Though I'm terrified of cancer, so I've given it up.

That went well.

Do you have children, Roger?

**ROGER.** Six.

**SANDY.** Oh my!

Did you hear that, Bookah?

You always wanted a sibling, and now you'll have six!

Be careful what you wish for.

I wished for Jesus' bones, and look at me now.

Help!

Jesus the janitor is half Muslim.

I don't know much about Muslims.

Or even half Muslims.

I'm confused.

Can someone give me info please?

Question mark.

Screw the smiley face.

Post.

WTF!

Is anyone out there?

I need info!

Where's my info?

Girls, run along.

Roger and I are desperate for alone time.

     *(to* **ROGER***)*

Got any condoms?

Just call me Fertile Myrtle.

Forty is the new thirty is the new twenty is the new ten.

And babies aren't my thing.

I prefer ponies.

Alas…

     *(A* **PONY** *trots across the stage.)*

**BECCA.** But I thought you were going through menopause.

**SANDY.** Peri-menopause.

Sad face.

One can still get pregnant.

As long as one still gets one's period.

Are you writing this down?

Becca?

Need a pen?

Lesson Two.

Your body will betray you.

Embrace it.

Delete.

Don't let yourself go.

Men are very visual.

You wouldn't understand.

You're a lesbian.

Lucky duck.

I have a wedgie.

Don't gloat.

Moms can too wear hot pants.

Says me.

That's who.

**BECCA.** Mom, can we talk for a sec?

This guy could be a serial killer.

You've never even met him.

**SANDY.** Don't be ridiculous.

Of course I've met him.

**ROGER.** I was her prom date.

**SANDY.** Back in 1985.

**ROGER.** I brought her a flower.

**SANDY.** He threw up on my shoes.

**ROGER.** No I didn't.

**SANDY.** Yes you did.

**BECCA.** That's disgusting.

**SANDY.** People change.

**BECCA.** You threw up on her shoes?

**ROGER.** I didn't throw up on her shoes.

**SANDY.** He was too drunk to remember.

**ROGER.** I gave up the sauce in 1996.

**SANDY.** He gave up the sauce in 1996.

**BECCA.** Then how come he's drinking champagne?

**SANDY.** Good point.

**ROGER.** If you must know the truth –

**SANDY.** I mustn't know the truth.

Keep the truth to yourself.

The truth is overrated.

**ROGER.** I'll drink to that.

**BECCA.** *(desperate)* I have an idea.

Why don't you two take a vacation?

See if you're compatible before you –

**SANDY.** Roger has asked me to marry him, and I have said yes.

Period.

End of story.

Now pack your bags.

We're moving to Ohio.

**BECCA.** Ohio?

**SANDY.** Yes, Ohio.

**ROGER.** Iowa, actually.

**SANDY.** Iowa?

**ROGER.** I live in Iowa.

**SANDY.** I thought Ohio.

**ROGER.** Nope, Iowa.

**SANDY.** What's in Iowa?

**ROGER.** Corn, cattle, caucuses, me.

**SANDY.** I'm a sucker for a caucus.

Say no more.

Enough said.

**BECCA.** But what about school?

**SANDY**. They have schools in Iowa.

    Don't they, Roger?

**ROGER**. I prefer to homeschool.

**SANDY**. Roger prefers to homeschool.

    What's the big deal?

    School is for suckers.

    You're your own best teacher.

    You'll be in college soon enough.

    What's a couple years in the span of a lifetime?

    A blip, Becca, a blip.

    You don't want me to die alone, do you?

**BECCA**. I guess not.

**SANDY**. To rot away in some urine soaked wheel chair.

    Covered in sores and feces.

    Neglected.

    Forgotten.

    Muttering incoherently.

    Buzzing for a nurse.

    Inhaling stale air and moldy potpourri.

    Howling like some rare type of monkey.

    Oo-ah.

    Don't do it, Becca.

    Don't stick me in a home.

    I'm your mother.

    Not a monkey.

    In a manner of speaking.

    Did I mention you're adopted?

    I'm mentioning it now.

    Baggy skin.

    Missing teeth.

    Denture cream.

    Diapers.

    You know I hate Jello.

    The consistency.

It's terrifying.

Take me to the woods and shoot me.

**BECCA.** OK.

**SANDY.** OK?

**BECCA.** Not a problem.

**SANDY.** You're the best.

I couldn't love you more than I do right now.

Well, unless you were a boy.

Or a pony.

You're not a pony...

*(A **PONY** trots across the stage.)*

**BECCA.** So I'm adopted?

**SANDY.** Duh.

**BECCA.** But I thought I was an accident.

**SANDY.** You were an accident.

**BECCA.** I don't get it.

**SANDY.** We adopted you by accident.

From a sad sack junkie with an acoustic guitar.

We were visiting Indonesia.

Teaching English to the blind.

You were the dirtiest little street urchin we ever did see.

How could we help but bring you home?

Give you a chance at a better life.

In America.

Home of the free.

Except for Muslims.

Who said that?

Jesus, get out of my head!

You're driving me mad!

All caps!

Where's my old self?

I miss my old self.

Has anybody seen my old self?

TTYL.

Refresh!

Roger?

**ROGER.** Yes, Sandy?

**SANDY.** Are you a Muslim?

**ROGER.** Nope.

**SANDY.** Phew.

Half a Muslim?

**ROGER.** Nope.

**SANDY.** Great.

Are you a janitor?

**ROGER.** Nope.

**SANDY.** Fab.

Half a janitor?

**ROGER.** Nope.

**SANDY.** Terrif.

Text me your address.

We'll be there in the blink of an eye.

Off to pack.

We should be there in time for Christmas.

Tra la la.

(**SANDY** *bumps into* **AMANDA** *on her way out.*)

**AMANDA.** Ouch!

**SANDY.** Amanda!

I'm thrilled to hear your voice.

And I mean that literally.

It's lovely.

Melodic.

How's your broken home?

Is it terribly abusive?

There there, Amanda.

Have a good cry.

Crying is healthy.

Let it all out.

How would you like a pony?

When I was a child, I longed for a pony.

Are you familiar with longing?

It's a feeling you get in the pit of your stomach, and there's no known cure.

Not even when you acquire the object of your longing.

How's that for irony?

Are you familiar with irony?

It's a three syllable word beginning with I.

Of all letters.

Much like Ohio.

**ROGER.** Iowa.

**AMANDA.** You can't move to Ohio.

**ROGER.** Iowa.

**AMANDA.** Bookah's my only friend.

Who am I gonna sit with at lunch?

**SANDY.** Lunch?

Who needs it?

Save yourself the calories.

Aren't you anorexic?

**AMANDA.** Bulemic.

**SANDY.** Think thin.

**AMANDA.** *(flattered)* Do I really look anorexic?

**SANDY.** You bet.

**AMANDA.** Are you for real?

**SANDY.** You could be in Auschwitz.

**AMANDA.** Auschwitz?

What's Auschwitz?

A fashion magazine?

**SANDY.** Well –

**AMANDA.** Like Vogue?

**SANDY.** Not exactly.

**AMANDA.** Teen Vogue?

**SANDY.** Where to begin?

**AMANDA.** Elle?

**SANDY**. You're better than Bookah.

Bookah writes poetry.

Just you wait, once Bookah's out of the picture, you'll have a million new friends.

Boys will be beating down your door.

If you play your cards right, you could be homecoming queen.

**AMANDA**. Homecoming queen?

That'll be the day!

I'm not exactly a cheerleader!

**SANDY**. So be a goddamn cheerleader!

**AMANDA**. But I'm a virgin.

**SANDY**. Says who?

**AMANDA**. And I can't do the splits.

**SANDY**. Anyone can do the splits.

Except for cripples and Bookah.

Don't worry your pretty little head.

**AMANDA**. Pretty?

Did you just call me pretty?

You should be a therapist.

I feel like a new person.

You just totally boosted my self esteem and body image.

**SANDY**. Happy to help.

Anything's possible if you have a little faith.

A little faith and perseverance.

Look at me and what's his name.

**ROGER**. Roger.

**AMANDA**. Have you guys set a date?

**SANDY**. February 14th.

**AMANDA**. Valentine's Day?

**SANDY**. You got it.

**AMANDA**. How romantic.

**SANDY**. Take it from me, it's never too late to start from scratch.

To shed your skin.

To face the day as a brand new you.

To turn your back on Jesus.

And renounce him.

Forever and ever.

Even though you long for his salvation.

Dear Diary.

What's a Muslim?

What's a half Muslim?

Who or what is Allah?

Maybe if I convert, Jesus will love me back.

Or better yet, I'll half convert.

If I had half a brain, I'd have been half a Muslim a long time ago.

What's a hijab?

What's a burqa?

Do Muslims eat pigs?

I like my bacon slightly burnt.

"Burnt food causes cancer."

What doesn't cause cancer?

Cancer runs in my family.

Should I be worried?

Hashtag.

Becca, buy me a burqa.

Try Amazon.

Dot com.

A burqa.

I said, a burqa.

And while you're at it, get me a Qur'an.

Preferably paperback.

My password is 'password.'

I know!

I know I have to change it.

You could have said that in a nicer tone.

Back off.

Take my Amex.

My Visa's maxed.

I can't get a loan.

I have creditors calling me day and night.

From India.

My savings are gone.

Why oh why did I buy this condo?

Why oh why did we invade that country?

I'm up to my knees in debt, sky high, and I need to find
a quick way out.

Any suggestions welcome.

Please don't flame me.

Happy Holidays.

**AMANDA.** You should totally become a therapist when you
move to Ohio.

**ROGER.** Iowa.

I live in Iowa.

**SANDY.** A therapist?

How do you figure?

It's not like I have a degree.

Heck, maybe I'll get a degree.

Heck, maybe I'll go back to school.

Heck, maybe I'll go back to sleep.

Heck, maybe I'll go back to stripping.

(as if reading)

"The best jobs for women over forty."

I'll figure it out!

**AMANDA.** Bye, Becca.

Bye, Mrs. Jones.

Bye, Bulimia.

Bye, ADD.

**SANDY.** Amanda, wait, before you run off.

How would you like to be my maid of honor?

**AMANDA.** I'd be honored.

**SANDY**. You're a hoot.

　　The pony I never had.

　　Here.

　　Take some hay.

　　For the road.

　　I insist.

**AMANDA**. Hay?

**SANDY**. No need to barf it up.

　　High fiber.

　　Low carbs.

　　You'll be pooping out your brains in no time.

　　Super filling.

**BECCA**. I have an announcement!

**SANDY**. No time for announcements!

　　Come along, Roger.

　　Don't dawdle.

　　Giddyup.

　　　　　*(**SANDY** exits with **ROGER**.)*

**BECCA**. I'm not moving to Iowa.

　　I'm moving to London.

**AMANDA**. London?

　　How can you move to London?

　　The only person you know in London is –

　　　　　*(**AMANDA** exits.)*

　　　　　*(Lights up on **JIM**'s flat in London. **JIM** and **LIZ**
　　　　　are in bed. **JIM** wakes up.)*

**JIM**. Hello?

**BECCA**. Dad?

**JIM**. There's no Dan here.

**BECCA**. I said Dad not Dan.

**JIM**. May I ask who's calling?

**BECCA**. Becca.

　　Your daughter.

**JIM**. What time is it?

**BECCA**. Seven here, so midnight there.

    I'm sorry to call so late, but –

**JIM**. How 'bout I ring you in the morning?

    They say 'ring' here in England.

    Did you know that, Becca?

    And they don't say 'cell phone', they say 'mobile'.

**LIZ**. Jim?

**JIM**. Sh.

**LIZ**. Who's calling?

**JIM**. My daughter.

**LIZ**. You didn't mention you had a daughter.

**JIM**. I'm mentioning it now.

**LIZ**. How old is she?

**JIM**. Twelve.

**BECCA**. I'm actually fourteen.

**LIZ**. Anything else you'd like to tell me before we walk down the aisle?

**JIM**. Where to begin?

    For starters…

    There's no such thing as a perfect man.

    I will travel to meet you.

    Or we can meet half way.

    I've got a thing for tortured souls.

**LIZ**. I'm a tortured soul.

**JIM**. You're my tortured soul.

**BECCA**. Dad, listen up –

**JIM**. I told you there's no Dan here.

**BECCA**. Mom's getting married.

**JIM**. Married?

    That's impossible.

    My mom's dead as a doornail.

    Doornails don't get married.

**BECCA.** Wait a minute.

  Grandma's dead?

**JIM.** April Fool's!

  Grandma's alive!

**BECCA.** It's the middle of December.

**JIM.** It's the middle of the night.

  How 'bout I ring you in the morning?

  They say 'ring' here in England.

  Did you know that Becca?

  And they don't say 'cell phone', they say 'mobile'.

**BECCA.** Let me start over.

  Mom's getting married.

**JIM.** My mom?

**BECCA.** No, mine.

  His name's Roger.

  He found her on Facebook.

  They were prom dates in 1985.

  He brought her a flower.

  He threw up on her shoes.

  And the thing is, he lives in Iowa, and she's making me
  move there, and –

    (**JIM** *snores. Just one snore.*)

  Dad, wake up!

  Mom's getting married.

**JIM.** (*quoting* Gone With The Wind)

  "Frankly my dear, I don't give a damn."

  Note to self:

  No more Ambien and Turner Classic Movies.

**LIZ.** What does she want exactly?

**JIM.** What do you *want* exactly?

**BECCA.** I want to live with you.

**JIM.** Live with me?

  She wants to live with me.

**LIZ.** Live with you?

**BECCA.** I won't be any trouble.

> I'll get a job.

> Pay rent.

> Before you know it, I'll go away to college.

**JIM.** OK!

**BECCA.** *(shocked)* OK?

**JIM.** Not a problem!

**BECCA.** You're the best.

**JIM.** *(sincere and excited)* I'd love to get reacquainted.

> Our Christmas tree is up.

> You can help with the finishing touches.

> We used to be so close, and now we're complete strangers.

> I feel like we're thousands of miles apart.

**BECCA.** *(confused)* We *are* thousands of miles apart.

**JIM.** Besides, I have an extra bedroom, so it shouldn't be a problem.

**LIZ.** Not for long.

**JIM.** What do you mean?

**LIZ.** Jim?

**JIM.** Liz?

**LIZ.** We're going to have a baby.

**JIM.** What?

**LIZ.** You're going to be a dad.

**JIM.** A dan?

**LIZ.** A dad.

> *(**LIZ** reveals her very pregnant belly.)*

**JIM.** Becca!

> Guess what?

> I'm going to be a dad!

> I guess you can't live with me after all.

> Drat.

> I always wanted to be a dad.

> Well, maybe not always.

Timing is everything.
So says Liz.
She's Chinese.
British born.

I'm called white.
Weird but true.
My skin color is pinkish beige.

Can we discuss this in the morning?
*Zai Jian.*
That's goodbye.
*Wan an.*
That's good night.
Mandarin is the language of tomorrow.
Here's why:

**BECCA.** Wait.

**JIM.** *(quoting* Taxi Driver*)* You talkin' to me?

**BECCA.** Dad, I have a question.

**JIM.** There *are* no stupid questions.

**BECCA.** Am I adopted?

**JIM.** Who wants to know?

**BECCA.** Me, I guess.

**JIM.** Well, in that case, yes.
We got you in Ohio.
Or was it Iowa?
Or Indonesia?
Purely accidental.
From a sad sack junkie with an acoustic guitar.
One can only hope she's in a better place.

**BECCA.** A better place?

**JIM.** Indonesia's sinking.
Global warming or hadn't you heard?
Rising sea levels.
Coastal erosion.

**BECCA.** Coastal erosion?

**JIM.** Sleep well.

   Liz, listen up.

   We were living overseas.

   Teaching English to the blind.

   She was the dirtiest little street urchin we ever did see.

   How could we help but bring her home?

   Give her a chance at a better life.

   In America.

   Home of the fat.

   Where's the beef?

   I love this country.

**LIZ.** But Jim, you're an expat.

**JIM.** I assure you I'm no expert.

**LIZ.** Expat.

   You're an expat.

**JIM.** Don't be silly.

   You're the expert.

**LIZ.** Expat.

**JIM.** I'm not an expert, but I play one on TV.

**BECCA.** Dad.

**JIM.** There's no Dan here.

**BECCA.** Expat.

   She said expat.

**JIM.** Help!

   I'm an expat!

   Living across the pond.

   England suits me to a tea.

   Not to mention a crumpet.

   I'm smitten with Britain.

   And they don't say daughter, they say 'doo-tuh'.

            (**LIZ** *grabs the phone.*)

**LIZ.** Your father's a wanker.

**BECCA.** What's a wanker?

**LIZ.** A sod.

**BECCA.** What's a sod?

**LIZ.** Why am I attracted to the wrong type of man?

**BECCA.** Tell me about it.

**LIZ.** Right?

**BECCA.** I'm in love with Mr. Hill.
He's my teacher.

**LIZ.** Sexy.

**BECCA.** Math.

**LIZ.** Numbers are *sexy*.
Tell him how you feel.
What have you got to lose?

**BECCA.** Try everything.

**LIZ.** Bollocks, grow a pair of bollocks, bollocks to the wall, man up, strap one on.

**BECCA.** How?

**LIZ.** Lipstick.
I always start with lipstick.

**BECCA.** I can't wear lipstick.

**LIZ.** Twaddle.

**BECCA.** I'm afraid.

**LIZ.** Dream big.

**BECCA.** What's twaddle?

**LIZ.** Poppycock.

**BECCA.** What's poppycock?

**LIZ.** Twaddle.

**BECCA.** You're officially insane.

**LIZ.** Actually, I'm an actuary.

**JIM.** Liz crunches my numbers.
Know what I mean?

**LIZ.** Lipstick!

**BECCA.** I don't have any lipstick.

**LIZ.** Do you have tinted Chapstick?

**BECCA.** Doubtful.

**LIZ**. Bloody hell.

> Blimey, blow me, suck it.
>
> Man the frig up.
>
> You're an orphan.

**BECCA**. I'm an orphan?

**LIZ**. Orphans are plucky.

**JIM**. *(takes the phone)* You rang?

**BECCA**. My birth mother's dead?

**JIM**. I'm so sorry for your loss.

**BECCA**. I was asking a question.

**JIM**. There are no stupid questions.

> If you happen to track her down, tell her I said hello.
>
> Tell her I changed careers.
>
> Tell her life is full of surprises.
>
> One day you're a pilot, and the next, you're a private eye.

**BECCA**. You changed careers?

**JIM**. Duh.

**BECCA**. You're a private eye?

**JIM**. Double duh.

> Check out my website.
>
> Still in beta, but we're improving.
>
> I'd love to hear your feedback.
>
> Shoot me an email.
>
> Or find me on Facebook.

**BECCA**. Since when are you on Facebook?

**JIM**. Since forever and a day.

> *(quoting* Taxi Driver*)*

> I've always depended on the kindness of Facebook friends.

**BECCA**. So, will you help me find my birth mother?

**JIM**. I'm not cheap.

**BECCA**. I have twenty seven dollars.

**JIM**. I charge top pound.

**LIZ.** Jim.

**JIM.** Not now. I'm on with a client.

**BECCA.** Let's talk about something else.

Let's talk about the tree house we never built.

That was fun.

**LIZ.** Feel.

He's kicking.

**JIM.** He's a he?

**BECCA.** I spent hours up there.

Me and the moon.

Reading Nancy Drew.

With a flashlight.

**LIZ.** Amazing.

**BECCA.** What do I want for Christmas?

**LIZ.** A brand new life.

**BECCA.** I guess I want to be a grown-up.

I want to live my own life.

Choose my own fate.

And also an iPhone.

And a mom who doesn't wear croptops.

I guess I want to be a kid again.

I want to sleep outside.

I don't care if I freeze.

I guess I want you to care if I freeze.

I guess I want you bring me a blanket.

Read me a book.

Sing me to sleep.

Whisper me to sleep.

Once upon a time, there was a girl.

She was normal.

**JIM.** Liz, why didn't you tell me?

**LIZ.** I was afraid.

**JIM.** No more secrets.

**LIZ.** Jim, why didn't you *tell* me.

**JIM.** I was ashamed.

**LIZ.** No more secrets.

**JIM.** I'm sorry.

**LIZ.** Don't cry.
I'm so sorry.

**JIM.** Please don't cry.
Sing to him in Mandarin.
Give him a leg up.
Sky's the limit.
You name it.

**LIZ.** Give him the whole world.

**BECCA.** What else?
Let me think.
I write poetry now.
Don't tell, OK?
Want to hear my latest?
I call it *Love is Bald:*
*An Ode to Mr. Hill.*
Ready?
Here goes.

## *[MUSIC NO. 2: "COASTAL EROSION"]*

**NANCY DREW.**
    COASTAL EROSION
    THE BEACH WEARS AWAY
    THE SPECTACULAR CITY IS
    IN DANGER OF FALLING

| **NANCY DREW.** | **COMPANY.** |
|---|---|
| COASTAL EROSION | MMM… |
| IS GRADUAL PLAY | |
| THE SPECTACULAR CITY IS | MMM |
| IN DANGER OF FALLING | MMM… |
| | |
| AND – WOW! – | WOW |
| THERE IT GOES ALL THE | |
| BUILDINGS AND PEOPLE | OOH |
| ALL THE HOUSEPETS AND | MMM |
| VEG'TABLE STANDS | |
| | |
| ALL THE GARDENS | OH… |
| AND FIREPLUGS | … |
| AND THE BOYS WITH | … |
| UN-HOLDABLE HANDS | … |
| LIKE A CUPFUL OF SAND | … |

**WIFE 4 / NANCY DREW.**
    IN THE BATHTUB
    ALL THE BATHTUBS!
    OH NO! OH NO!

    AND NOW IT LOOKS LIKE
    A BIG SLICE OF CAKE
    SUDDENLY SLICED AND EXPOSED
    HOW EMBARRASSING.
    THOSE WET INNER LAYERS.
    THOSE EDIBLE INSIDES.

| **NANCY DREW.** | **COMPANY.** |
|---|---|
| DON'T LOOK | OH… OH… |
| **NANCY DREW & BECCA.** | |
| DON'T LOOK | OH… OH… OH… |

**NANCY DREW.**

COASTAL EROSION
WAS KINDA PRETTY
WHEN IT WAS GRADUAL
WHEN IT WAS GRADUAL

(**BECCA** *is in a tree house.*)

(*She is seven years old.*)

(*Her father stands at the foot of the tree.*)

(*This scene has a different tone: real, slow, spacious, heartfelt.*)

(**JIM** *is a dad who wants to connect with his daughter.*)

**JIM.** *(yelling up to her)* Becca!

　　Come inside!

　　It's cold!

**YOUNGER BECCA.** *(yelling down)* I have a blanket.

**JIM.** Five minutes.

　　That's it.

**YOUNGER BECCA.** One more chapter.

**JIM.** Coming up.

　　Hi.

**YOUNGER BECCA.** Hi.

**JIM.** What are you reading?

　　　　*(small pause)*

**YOUNGER BECCA.** Nancy Drew.

**JIM.** You need more light?

**YOUNGER BECCA.** I'm fine.

**JIM.** You sure?

　　Your eyes…

　　Some tree house…

　　Place looks great.

**YOUNGER BECCA.** You know what we need is a telescope.

**JIM.** Your birthday's coming up.

**YOUNGER BECCA.** I want to see Mars.

**JIM.** Mars is *small.*

**YOUNGER BECCA.** My birthday's a million years away.

**JIM.** Eight years old.

**YOUNGER BECCA.** Why is Mars red?

**JIM.** Because of iron.

Essentially.

Rust.

> *(beat)*

**YOUNGER BECCA.** Dad?

**JIM.** You name it.

**YOUNGER BECCA.** How do you know everything?

**JIM.** Sky's the limit.

For example...

Let's just say...

> *(trails off)*

So, what's up with Nancy?

**YOUNGER BECCA.** She found a diary.

**JIM.** Huh.

**YOUNGER BECCA.** But she can't understand it because it's in another language.

**JIM.** Want me to read to you a little?

**YOUNGER BECCA.** Out loud?

**JIM.** Never mind.

How's school?

Who's your best friend these days?

Still Nancy?

Don't you want a real best friend?

**YOUNGER BECCA.** Nancy has a convertible.

A mustang.

It's blue.

She got it for her birthday.

When she turned eighteen.

From her dad.

He's a lawyer.

Her mother died.

**JIM.** That's too bad.

**YOUNGER BECCA.** She has a boyfriend.

He's in college.

Ned.

**JIM.** Plenty of time for that later.

**YOUNGER BECCA.** He plays baseball, basketball, and football.

Why are you a pilot?

I said, why are you pilot?

**JIM.** I guess I used to be a kid who dreamed of flying a plane.

**YOUNGER BECCA.** Do you like being a pilot?

**JIM.** Sometimes.

Sure.

Everyone likes the sky.

Know what I mean?

**LIZ.** *(referring to her baby)* Jim!

It's time!

**JIM.** Sets you free.

**LIZ.** Let's go!

**BECCA.** I guess I used to be a kid who dreamed of Mars. ·

### [MUSIC NO. 3: "JESUS' BONES / SHOULD I BE WORRIED"]

**LIZ.**

JESUS'S BONES
ARE JUST LIKE YOURS
BUT, OH, JESUS'S EYES!
OH, JESUS'S EYES!
THERE ARE JUST SOME THINGS THAT
YOU'LL JUST NEVER BE
NO MATTER HOW HARD YOU TRY
NO MATTER HOW HARD YOU TRY

JUMP, JUMP, JUMP LITTLE BABY
JUMP, JUMP, JUMP LITTLE GUY
HEAVEN AND EARTH DO NOT TOUCH ONE ANOTHER
BUT JUMP, JUMP, JUMP, JUMP UP AND TRY

DON'T CRY

Don't cry.

| **LIZ.** | **CHEERLEADER.** |
|---|---|
| JESUS'S BONES ARE | WILL MY DEODORANT GIVE ME ALZHEIMER'S? WHAT'S THE RISK? IS |
| JUST LIKE YOURS, BUT | WIFI HARMFUL TO MY HEALTH? SHOULD I BE WORRIED? |
| OH, JESUS'S | ON A SCALE OF ONE TO TEN HOW WORRIED SHOULD I BE? |
| HANDS. | ABOUT ALL THE EVIL MEN IN THE WORLD? ABOUT |
| OH, JESUS'S | CLIMATE CHANGE ABOUT CHEMICALS LEACHING TO MY FOOD WHEN I |
| HANDS | USE A PLASTIC CONTAINER? ABOUT SULFITES AND NITRATES AND |
| YOU'LL NEVER SAVE ONE | GMO INGREDIENTS? |

| | AND WATER FROM THE TAP |
| --- | --- |
| | AND THE |
| SINGLE SOUL, NO | AIR AND THE FISH? |
| | AND SCREEN TIME |
| | HOW MUCH IS TOO |
| MATTER HOW HARD YOU | MUCH? |
| | WHAT IS BPA? |
| | WHAT ARE PARABENS? |
| | WHAT'S THE RISK? |
| TRY AND BE- | HOW WORRIED SHOULD I BE? |
| | ABOUT A CREDIT CHECK? |
| -LIEVE ME, YOU'RE | ABOUT HPV? |
| GONNA | ABOUT HOW I BEHAVED IN |
| | THE '90S? |
| TRY | ABOUT HOW I BEHAVED IN |
| JUMP, JUMP, | THE '80S? |
| JUMP LITTLE BABY | ARE EGGS GOOD OR BAD FOR |
| | MY CHOLESTEROL? IS |
| JUMP, JUMP | COFFEE GOOD OR BAD FOR |
| | MY DIABETES? |
| JUMP LITTLE GUY | SHOULD I BE WORRIED |
| | ABOUT MY CHILD'S |
| | NIGHTMARES |
| HEAVEN AND EARTH DO | ABOUT MY CHILD'S |
| NOT | NOSEBLEEDS? AM I A |
| TOUCH ONE ANOTHER | BAD PERSON |
| BUT | IF I DRIVE AN SUV? |
| | WHY DO MY EARS RING |
| JUMP JUMP | AND MY EYELIDS TWITCH? |
| | WILL I GET BREAST CANCER IF |
| | I CARRY MY CELL PHONE |
| JUMP JUMP UP AND | IN MY BRA? |
| | I'M KINDA FREAKING |
| | OUT ABOUT THE RISE OF |
| | SUPERBUGS |

**CHEERLEADER.**

AND THE RISE OF CYBERBULLIES

AND FRACKING

AND SWINE FLU

AND BIRD FLU

AND THE STAGNANT POND A QUARTER MILE AWAY

AND RETIREMENT

AND MATERNITY LEAVE

AND BIKINI SEASON

I'M TURNING FORTY-FIVE

I'M TURNING SIXTEEN NEXT WEEK

I'M TURNING THIRTY AND STILL SINGLED
OH OH

I'M TURNING INTO MY MOTHER
I'M WORRIED ABOUT MY KIDS.
I'M STILL WORRIED ABOUT MY KIDS.
I GUESS I'M STILL WORRIED ABOUT MY KIDS.

Why is my snot green?

OH

Should I be worried at this point or should I just sit tight?
OH.
Is this something that I should keep an eye on?

MMMMM.

*(**SANDY** sits at her lap top, wearing a burqa.)*

*(**BECCA** enters, on her way to school.)*

**SANDY.** Becca!

You scared me!

I thought I was alone.

Alone online.

Online alone.

My online community is a ghost town.

You're up early.

What's new?

Same old, same old?

My burqa arrived from Amazon!

Takes some getting used to.

What do you think?

I'm on the fence.

Jury's still out.

Upshot:

No more sunblock.

**BECCA.** You can't wear a burqa.

It's offensive.

**SANDY.** To whom?

**BECCA.** To me.

**SANDY.** Be specific.

**BECCA.** To Muslims.

To half-Muslims.

**SANDY.** Can't you be specific?

**BECCA.** To humans.

**SANDY.** *(taking off the burqa)* You're right.

You're absolutely right.

Even a stopped clock…

I would hate to offend the humans.

I'll send it back.

What was I thinking?

Excellent question!

           *(**SANDY** has taken off the burqa to reveal something*
           *slutty, like a crop top.)*

**BECCA.** Mom, oh my god, put the burqa back on!

**SANDY.** I just can't win with you, can I?!

    Burqa, don't just stand there.

    Help me with my Becca.

    My Becca's stuck.

    Thank you, Burqa.

           *(**SANDY** has put the burqa back on.)*

    You look different.

**BECCA.** I am different.

**SANDY.** Want some breakfast?

**BECCA.** Just coffee.

**SANDY.** Coffee?

    Not my Burqa.

    My Burqa hates coffee.

**BECCA.** I love coffee.

**SANDY.** Since when?

**BECCA.** Since now.

**SANDY.** Lesson Three.

    Coffee stunts your growth.

**BECCA.** That's a myth.

**SANDY.** You're a handful!

**BECCA.** I'm basically fully grown.

**SANDY.** Don't sell yourself short.

    Get it?

**BECCA.** No!

**SANDY.** Who do you think you are and what have you done
with Burqa?

    Will the real Burqa Jones please stand up?

    Fine, I'll bite.

**BECCA.** Did you know Dad's a private eye?

**SANDY.** He died of cancer.

My dad.

**BECCA.** He's getting married.

**SANDY.** That reminds me.

So am I!

**BECCA.** Her name's Liz.

She's a wanker.

**SANDY.** Dear Diary,

Will you walk me down the aisle.

Thanks, D.

By the way, Burqa's acting weird.

**BECCA.** She crunches numbers.

**SANDY.** Don't be vulgar.

**BECCA.** They had a baby.

It's a boy.

**SANDY.** What's a boy?

Burqa, you never tell me anything.

**BECCA.** They're traveling the world.

Teaching Mandarin to the blind.

**SANDY.** We used to be so close and now we're complete
strangers.

*(texting Jesus)*

I feel like we're thousands of miles apart.

**BECCA.** What are you doing?

**SANDY.** Texting Jesus.

It's like sexting.

But with a T.

*(to BECCA)*

Do I have to wear my Becca when I spin.

I wonder…

I suppose I could hem my Becca.

Burqa, do you sew?

**BECCA.** Gotta go.

Wish me luck.

**SANDY.** Good luck!

What for?

**BECCA.** I'm facing the day as a brand new me.

**SANDY.** But I like the old you.

**BECCA.** Since when?

**SANDY.** Since now.

Are you wearing lipstick?

**BECCA.** Tinted chapstick.

**SANDY.** Take it off.

You look like a clown.

Big day!

Today!

Your last day of school before Ohio!

**BECCA.** Iowa.

**SANDY.** *(desperate)* How do you take your coffee?

**BECCA.** To go.

One Splenda.

**SANDY.** *(desperate)* Splenda?

Not my burqa!

My burqa hates Splenda!

# PART II

## SCHOOL

*[MUSIC NO. 4 "CHEERLEADERS"]*

**AMANDA.**

> CHEERLEADERS ARE HEALTHY EATERS
> CHEERLEADERS ARE NAT'RALLY OCCURRING
> PARAGONS OF STYLE AND SOCIAL EASE!
> OH, OH
> WHEN THEIR KNEES BEND,
> ANTICIPATION SEIZES US.
> OH! OH
> OH, WHAT LEAP OR KICK
> OR PYRAMID

> *(The rest of the* **COMPANY** *stomps and claps along.)*

> AM I ABOUT TO WITNESS?
> WILL IT BE SO PERFECT
> THAT IT FINALLY MAKES ME BELIEVE IN GOD?

| **AMANDA, BECCA, LIZ.** | **COMPANY.** |
|---|---|
| | RAH RAH RAH! |
| | RAH RAH RAH! |
| OH… | RAH RAH RAH! |
| | RAH RAH RAH! |
| OH… OH, OH | GO TEAM GO! |
| OH… OH… | GO, VICTORY! |
| … | FIGHT FIGHT WIN! GO |
| OH… OH… | GO WIN! GO WIN! |
| OH… | RAH RAH RAH! |
| OH… | RAH RAH RAH! |
| OH… OH! OH | GO WIN! |

**AMANDA.**

> CHEERLEADERS ARE HEALTHY EATERS
> CHEERLEADERS ARE PERFECTLY COMPORTED,
> PARADISE IS SURELY LITTERED WITH POM POMS.
> NOT TO MENTION PROM.

AND ... MY MOM
WAS A CHEERLEADER ALSO.

CHEERLEADERS ARE HEALTHY EATERS.

(**AMANDA** *stares at a* **CHEERLEADER**.)

**CHEERLEADER**. Stare much?

**AMANDA**. Ouch!

**CHEERLEADER**. What's your problem?

**AMANDA**. I dropped my hay.

**CHEERLEADER**. So I'm a cheerleader.

So my legs are freakin' toned.

So what?

So my abs are freakin' cut.

I'm still a person.

I still have feelings, OK?

Quit staring.

We're both girls.

You're creeping me out.

**AMANDA**. Sorry.

**CHEERLEADER**. No worries.

Free country.

I get it.

This is America.

Why are you eating hay?

**AMANDA**. High fiber.

Fills you up.

**CHEERLEADER**. Does it have dairy?

I'm off dairy.

Gives me zits, OK?

Gives me zits and sweaty pits.

So sue me, OK?

So I have flaws and imperfections.

So I'm human, OK?

Stop staring at my boobs.

So I'm blessed with a nice rack.

So my body attracts danger.

I'm not a sex object, OK?

I'm just a girl with random talents.

**CHEERLEADER.** *(cont.)* I want to be *serious.*
Seriously.
I want to be taken seriously.
I'm serious.
Thank you, Jesus.

I'm not complaining.

News flash:
Cheerleaders are people too.
We're just like everyone else.
We have 'hopes, dreams, and fears'.
We like to do stuff.

**AMANDA.** I like to do stuff.

**CHEERLEADER.** We like jeans.

**AMANDA.** I like jeans.

**CHEERLEADER.** How old are you?

**AMANDA.** Fourteen.

**CHEERLEADER.** Can you shut up?
Wanna get high?

*(They get high.)*

**AMANDA.** He has herpes.
FYI.

**CHEERLEADER.** Who?

**AMANDA.** Jesus.

**CHEERLEADER.** Big deal.
Lots of people have herpes.

**AMANDA.** Jesus isn't a person.

**CHEERLEADER.** Freak show.
Only kidding.
You're not a freak show.

**AMANDA.** Want some hay?

**CHEERLEADER.** Gross.

**AMANDA.** You get used to it.

**CHEERLEADER.** Gimme.

**AMANDA.** *(discovery)* I'm not a freak show.

**CHEERLEADER.** Lots of people have herpes.

It's kind of a rite of passage.

Like date rape…

**AMANDA.** This is America…

**CHEERLEADER.** Cheerleaders are people too.

We're just like everyone else.

We like to save the planet by going green.

**AMANDA.** I like green.

I could be in Auschwitz.

**CHEERLEADER.** Are you Jewish?

**AMANDA.** Bulemic.

Me.

On the cover of Auschwitz.

Ask my therapist.

　　　　*(beat)*

**CHEERLEADER.** I have a brother.

He's different.

**AMANDA.** My brother's overseas.

**CHEERLEADER.** Hawaii?

Sweet.

**AMANDA.** Afghanistan.

**CHEERLEADER.** Sucks.

Are you a proud American?

**AMANDA.** Same.

I have a stepdad.

**CHEERLEADER.** My half sister hates me.

Whatever.

**AMANDA.** I'm different.

**CHEERLEADER.** My friends call me 'Genius' because I'm…

not.

　　　　*(beat)*

**AMANDA.** Jesus, was he a janitor?

**CHEERLEADER.** I think he was a carpenter.

**AMANDA.** Jesus was half janitor, half carpenter.

**CHEERLEADER.** Deal.

**AMANDA.** Are you high?

I think I'm high.

Are you high?

I think I'm high.

What does high feel like?

**CHEERLEADER.** Happy.

No gravity.

Relaxed.

Hope for peace.

**AMANDA.** You know what I hate is Christmas.

**CHEERLEADER.** Christmas?

Been there, done that.

What's not to hate?

**AMANDA.** Do I look Jewish?

I'm not Italian.

I like pizza.

Do I look Greek?

I'm not middle eastern.

**CHEERLEADER.** Calm down.

So I'm a Cheerleader.

So I can do a standing backflip on a concrete sidewalk.

No I won't show you.

Such a natural feeling...

Indescribable...

Just...

Flows...

You sure it doesn't have dairy?

**AMANDA.** Pretty sure.

**CHEERLEADER.** Confession:

Jeans make me sad.

My favorite color is blue.

Because blue is sea and sky.

I like the sky.

Because it's endless.

And then it gets dark.

AMANDA. My favorite color is blue.

Except for jeans.

I like the sky.

It changes from blue to pink.

And then it gets dark.

CHEERLEADER. Text me if you want to hang out.

AMANDA. Hope for peace.

*(They exit.)*

### *[MUSIC NO. 5: "THIS IS AMERICA"]*

**LIZ.**

> THIS IS AMERICA.
> I LOVE THIS COUNTRY.
> I LOVE THE FOUNDING FATHERS

**LIZ, AMANDA, CHEERLEADER, NANCY DREW.**

> AND THE DREAM
> OF MARTIN LUTHER KING JUNIOR
> AND THE GRAND CANYON
> AND THE GRAND TETONS
> AND GRAND CENTRAL STATION
> AND THE WIDE OPEN SPACES

**LIZ.**

> AND THE FIRST AMENDMENT

**LIZ, AMANDA, CHEERLEADER, NANCY DREW.**

> AND THE FIRST LADY

**LIZ.**

> AND THE FLAG

*(MR. HILL's classroom.)*

*(MR. HILL has fallen asleep at his desk.)*

*(BECCA watches him sleep.)*

*(MR. HILL wakes up.)*

MR. HILL. Becca.

BECCA. Mr. Hill.

MR. HILL. How long have you been standing there?

BECCA. Literally?

Seven minutes.

Metaphorically.

All year.

MR. HILL. Shoot.

I have to run.

I must have dozed off.

BECCA. I came to say goodbye.

MR. HILL. I'm late for an appointment.

Happy holidays.

Have a nice break.

BECCA. Goodbye forever.

I'm moving.

MR. HILL. Moving?

Oh no.

I hadn't heard.

BECCA. Well, it's true.

MR. HILL. I'm sorry to hear that.

BECCA. How sorry exactly?

MR. HILL. You've been a pleasure to have in class.

You're bright.

Hard-working.

All your teachers would agree.

BECCA. Let's leave them out of this, shall we?

*(BECCA hands MR. HILL a small Christmas tree in a flower pot.)*

**BECCA.** Here.

**MR. HILL.** What's this?

**BECCA.** A parting gift.

**MR. HILL.** How thoughtful.

**BECCA.** In case you start to forget me.

As you can see we share a resemblance.

We're both odd-shaped and prickly.

Plus we like to be left alone.

Beautiful on the inside –

*(desperate)*

Wait!

**MR. HILL.** *(exasperated)* What's up?

**BECCA.** Why aren't you married?

I said, why aren't you married?

**MR. HILL.** How do you know I'm not married?

**BECCA.** Who is she?

I'll kill her.

**MR. HILL.** Let's just say I'm married to Math, OK?

**BECCA.** Math is stupid.

**MR. HILL.** Take it back.

**BECCA.** I take it back.

Numbers are sexy.

I want to crunch your numbers.

**MR. HILL.** Becca, moving is difficult.

Especially in the middle of the year.

I should know.

I was an army brat.

**BECCA.** Boo hoo for you.

**MR. HILL.** You'll have to start a new school.

Make new friends.

**BECCA.** Actually, I'm being homeschooled.

**MR. HILL.** I went to five different high schools.

**BECCA.** Cry me a river.

>  (*rubbing her pointer and thumb together*)

What's this?

The world's smallest violin.

**MR. HILL.** So, where are you moving?

And when?

**BECCA.** What's with the third degree?

**MR. HILL.** I care about my students.

**BECCA.** I'm not your student anymore.

I'm your lover.

**MR. HILL.** You're not my lover.

**BECCA.** Pretend I'm Math.

Pure and elegant.

Like a proof.

A beautiful proof.

Exquisitely constructed.

The most breathtaking of proofs.

Pretend that's me.

Forget it.

I'm aware it's a stretch.

**MR. HILL.** Becca, I'm flattered, but I could be your father.

**BECCA.** Are you from Indonesia?

I was adopted from Indonesia.

From a sad sack junkie with an acoustic guitar.

**MR. HILL.** You don't look Indonesian.

**BECCA.** (*pissed*) Are you calling me fat?

**MR. HILL.** Becca, if you'll excuse me, I have to get going.

**BECCA.** Hot date with Math?

**MR. HILL.** Very funny.

**BECCA.** Who's laughing?

**MR. HILL.** But I wish you the very best.

I really do.

**BECCA.** Gee thanks.

**MR. HILL.** You're one of my strongest students.

**BECCA.** One of?

That's bullshit.

Who's better than me?

**MR. HILL.** Better than *I*.

**BECCA.** *(swooning)* Touché.

Wait.

Are you gay?

Just my luck.

Of course you're gay.

I guess I could use a gay best friend.

How 'bout it, Mr. Hill?

What should we do first?

Do you like shopping?

**MR. HILL.** I'm forty-three.

**BECCA.** I'm an old soul.

Besides, my mom says forty is the new ten.

Help!

I'm in love with my gay best friend!

And it's unbearable!

A poem by Becca Jones.

Psst… I'm a poet.

Don't tell, OK?

My love is unraveling.

Like a giant ball of yarn.

I love everything about you.

Even the scar on your arm.

What happened?

**MR. HILL.** None of your business.

Tattoo.

Got it removed.

**BECCA.** Tattoo of what?

**MR. HILL.** A hawk.

**BECCA.** You like hawks?!

**MR. HILL.** Not anymore.

As I was saying, I wish you the best of luck.

**BECCA.** As I was saying, gee thanks.

**MR. HILL.** You've got a real knack for geometry.

**BECCA.** Really?

Do you think so?

Do you think I'm going to go places?

Make a difference in the world?

I've got my whole life ahead of me, right, Mr. Hill?

**MR. HILL.** Sure thing.

**BECCA.** Dream big.

**MR. HILL.** See you later.

**BECCA.** *(desperate)* What's the rush?

**MR. HILL.** I'm late, OK?

I have an appointment, OK?

**BECCA.** With who?

**MR. HILL.** With whom.

**BECCA.** With your shrink?

**MR. HILL.** With my daughter.

**BECCA.** Daughter?

What daughter?

You don't have a daughter.

**MR. HILL.** Yes, I do.

**BECCA.** No, you don't.

**MR. HILL.** Actually, I do.

**BECCA.** Actually, you don't.

**MR. HILL.** Becca, I do.

**BECCA.** Mr. Hill, you don't.

**MR. HILL.** *(losing his temper)* You know what?

You're right.

You're absolutely right.

I don't have a daughter.

Her name isn't Samantha.

She doesn't live in Florida.

**MR. HILL.** *(cont.)* With her mom.

  Who doesn't hate me.

  Samantha isn't twelve.

  She doesn't like gymnastics.

  She doesn't like her stepdad.

  More than me.

  She isn't spoiled.

  She doesn't play the drums.

  She doesn't have my eyes.

  She isn't changing.

  Every minute.

  Every day.

  Without me.

  We don't Skype.

  Every Friday.

  At four o'clock.

> *(looks at his watch)*

  Shit.

  And I don't have a first name.

  My parents named me Mister.

**BECCA.** Maybe you *should* see a shrink.

**MR. HILL.** Excellent idea.

  You want to pay for it?

  Great!

  I'll send you the bill.

> *(beat)*

**BECCA.** Wow!

**MR. HILL.** What's your problem?

**BECCA.** Nothing.

  Oh nothing.

  It's just I never would have pegged you for a deadbeat dad.

**MR. HILL.** What can I tell you?

  Looks can be deceiving.

**BECCA.** Lesson learned.

I'm sorry things ended so badly.

Bye, Mr. Hill.

Have a nice life.

**MR. HILL.** *(mean)* Bye, Becca.

Have fun dreaming big.

Seriously.

I hope your dreams don't crash and burn.

**BECCA.** *(meaner)* Have fun being middle aged.

**MR. HILL.** *(meanest)* Have fun being beautiful on the inside.

**BECCA.** *(deeply wounded)* Sticks and stones.

I'm taking back my Christmas tree.

And I'm throwing away my ode.

Love is not bald like a bald eagle in the air.

Love has a lustrous and full head of hair.

And Math is retarded.

Like you.

'TARD!

**MR. HILL.** Very mature.

**BECCA.** And love isn't ageless.

Love is young.

Like the night.

**MR. HILL.** Good luck with your poetry.

**BECCA.** We can't all be Math teachers.

**MR. HILL.** You don't know anything about me.

**BECCA.** I know your parents named you Mister.

I know you used to like hawks.

I know your daughter hates your guts.

Make that your doo-tuh.

**MR. HILL.** What's a doo-tuh?

**BECCA.** Would you like me to continue?

**MR. HILL.** Leave me alone!

**BECCA.** Army brat!

I know you're spending Christmas by yourself!

*(MR. HILL throws the Christmas tree.)*

**MR. HILL.** This is not how I pictured my life!

**BECCA.** Shocker!

**MR. HILL.** High school might suck.

But real life is even worse.

**BECCA.** My life is real.

My life is just as real as yours.

*(NANCY DREW drives up in her roadster.)*

**BLACK NANCY DREW.** Beep beep.

**BECCA.** Nancy Drew?

**MR. HILL.** Stupid kid.

Just you wait.

You don't have a clue.

**BLACK NANCY DREW.** Nancy Drew has loads of clues.

**BECCA.** Go away.

**MR. HILL.** Nice roadster.

**BLACK NANCY DREW.** Thanks, Mister.

**BECCA.** Hey, how do you know his name?

**BLACK NANCY DREW.** Nancy Drew knows everything.

I can paint like Picasso and ride like a cowboy.

Dance like Ginger Rogers and ski like a pro.

Solve any mystery in a hundred and eighty pages.

How do you like my twin-set?

Dressing well will open any door.

Even one connected to a top secret factory.

Plus I'm black now.

**BECCA.** Huh?

**BLACK NANCY DREW.** I got a makeover.

Can't you tell?

I also come in Asian.

And Latina.

And Jewish.

You have to stay relevant.

Appeal to a wider market.

If you want to stay afloat in this economy.

Progress!

The world's changing fast.

Are you?

Hey gang.

> (ASIAN, LATINA, *and* JEWISH NANCY DREWS
> *have entered.*)

**ALL NANCY DREWS.** Hi-de-ho.

We came to help you find your birth mother.

**BECCA.** Get out of my face.

**ALL NANCY DREWS.** What's eating her?

**MR. HILL.** Becca's moving to Iowa.

**BECCA.** Am not!

**MR. HILL.** Are too!

**ALL NANCY DREWS.** Bon voyage, Bookah.

**BECCA.** Hey, how do you know my name?

**ALL NANCY DREWS.** Bon voyage, Burqa.

**BECCA.** Hey, how do you know my other name?

**MR. HILL.** Burqa?

**ASIAN NANCY DREW.** Bookah?

**BLACK NANCY DREW.** Burqa?

**BECCA.** Becca!

**LATINA NANCY DREW.** Boo-kah?

**JEWISH NANCY DREW.** Bookah.

**ASIAN NANCY DREW.** Burqa?

**MR. HILL.** Bookah?

**LATINA NANCY DREW.** Burqa?

**BECCA.** Who am I?

Where am I?

**BLACK NANCY DREW.** Jeepers creepers.

**JEWISH NANCY DREW.** *Oy gevalt.*

**LATINA NANCY DREW.** *Dios mio.*

ASIAN NANCY DREW. *Wo de tian a.*

BLACK NANCY DREW. You used to be so cute.

ASIAN NANCY DREW. Adorable.

    Up in the tree house.

JEWISH NANCY DREW. You were a bubbeleh.

ASIAN NANCY DREW. You were a doll.

LATINA NANCY DREW. *Una muchacha tan bonita.*

ASIAN NANCY DREW. Such a pity.

JEWISH NANCY DREW. Such a shame.

LATINA NANCY DREW. *¿Qué pasó?*

MR. HILL. Mustang, right?

BLACK NANCY DREW. Got it for my birthday.

MR. HILL. Lucky you.

BLACK NANCY DREW. I'll say.

    My dad's a handsome lawyer.

BECCA. Mr. Hill's a middle-aged math teacher.

BLACK NANCY DREW. Sorry, Charlie.

    I'll always be eighteen.

    Only now I'm multi-culti.

    And I'm hot.

        *(The* NANCY DREWS *do a sizzle gesture.)*

        *(*MR. HILL*'s cell phone rings.)*

MR. HILL. Excuse me, I have to take this.

BECCA. Samantha?

MR. HILL. India.

BECCA. Don't be a stranger.

        *(*MR. HILL *exits.)*

BLACK NANCY DREW. Ned's thrilled with my new boobs.

ASIAN NANCY DREW. Can't believe his luck.

LATINA NANCY DREW. Always wants to go to second base.

JEWISH NANCY DREW. Rascal.

BECCA. I'm so sick of Nancy Drew I could vomit.

**BLACK NANCY DREW.** Say, are you a racist?

Admit it.

You're a racist.

**BECCA.** Of course I'm not a racist.

I hate everyone.

**BLACK NANCY DREW.** Confession:

I used to be a racist until my makeover.

News flash:

Skin color doesn't matter if you have a rich dad.

**ASIAN NANCY DREW.** And triple Ds.

**LATINA NANCY DREW.** And a boyfriend.

**JEWISH NANCY DREW.** And an iPhone 6.

**BECCA.** No way.

You have an iPhone 6?!

I hate your guts.

**JEWISH NANCY DREW.** Anti-semite.

**LATINA NANCY DREW.** Later gator.

Off to the haunted mansion.

**JEWISH NANCY DREW.** Catch ya later, Street Urchin.

**ASIAN NANCY DREW.** *Zai Jian.*

**BECCA.** But what about my birth mother?

**ALL NANCY DREWS.** Get out of my face!

> (**ASIAN, LATINA,** *and* **JEWISH NANCY DREWS** *exit.*)

**BLACK NANCY DREW.** Don't be cross.

Turkey's got you down?

*Parlez-vous français?*

Are you sure you're not a racist?

Cry-baby.

**BECCA.** Take your stupid convertible and shove it up your –

**BLACK NANCY DREW.** Black ass?

**BECCA.** What?

I didn't say that.

**BLACK NANCY DREW.** Maybe you didn't say it but you *thought* it.

**BECCA.** No I didn't.

You don't know anything.

**BLACK NANCY DREW.** I'm your celebrity idol.

**BECCA.** You're not a celebrity.

**BLACK NANCY DREW.** I'm famous.

**BECCA.** You don't even exist.

Not in real life.

**BLACK NANCY DREW.** Real life is boring.

**BECCA.** Not as boring as you.

I outgrew you, like, a hundred million years ago.

**BLACK NANCY DREW.** Yeah right.

I'm your girl crush.

**BECCA.** I don't have a girl crush.

**BLACK NANCY DREW.** Why not?

Homophobic?

Homophobic much?

**BECCA.** Hello!

I have a gay best friend!

What's wrong?

**BLACK NANCY DREW.** I thought *I* was your best friend.

**BECCA.** You are!

Don't cry!

You are my best friend!

**BLACK NANCY DREW.** Am I your gay best friend?

**BECCA.** You're gay?

*(TRANSGENDER NANCY DREW enters.)*

**TRANSGENDER NANCY DREW.** Transgender.

**BECCA.** *(interested)* She's transgender?

**BLACK NANCY DREW.** *They're* transgender.

**TRANSGENDER NANCY DREW.** Call me *they*.

**BECCA.** Hi, They!

See you later, They!

*(TRANSGENDER NANCY DREW exits.)*

**BLACK NANCY DREW.** You outgrew me.

**BECCA.** No I didn't.

**BLACK NANCY DREW.** You said you outgrew me.

**BECCA.** I was kidding.

I was lying.

I didn't outgrow you.

I could *never* outgrow you.

**BLACK NANCY DREW.** Am I boring?

**BECCA.** Nancy Drew?

You're the opposite of boring.

**BLACK NANCY DREW.** What's the opposite of boring?

**BECCA.** Fun!

**BLACK NANCY DREW.** I'm fun!

Swear on a stack of bibles!

**BECCA.** I swear on a stack of bibles!

I can't believe you're crying.

**BLACK NANCY DREW.** Celebrities are people too.

**BECCA.** You're my celebrity idol.

**BLACK NANCY DREW.** Darn tootin'!

**BECCA.** You're my girl crush!

**BLACK NANCY DREW.** Swear on a stack of babies!

Fuck a doodle doo!

**BECCA.** You're my BFF!

Forget Amanda!

**BLACK NANCY DREW.** Who's Amanda?!

**BECCA.** Amanda never talks to me anyway!

**BLACK NANCY DREW.** You shouldn't gossip.

**BECCA.** Sorry.

**BLACK NANCY DREW.** Gossip is a sin.

**BECCA.** You're right.

**BLACK NANCY DREW.** Am I right?

**BECCA.** Nancy Drew is always –

**BLACK NANCY DREW.** White?

**BECCA.** What?

   I didn't say that.

**BLACK NANCY DREW.** Maybe you didn't say it but you thought it.

**BECCA.** No I didn't.

**BLACK NANCY DREW.** If you don't have anything nice to say, don't say anything at all.

   I quote the Bible.

**BECCA.** Which book?

**BLACK NANCY DREW.** The book of Nancy.

   Snap!

**BECCA.** Nancy Drew is Catholic.

   She doesn't joke about the Bible.

**BLACK NANCY DREW.** How do you know I'm Catholic?

   Stalker.

   A bible walks into a bar.

   What did the bible say to the bible?

   Why did the bible cross the road?

**BECCA.** Why?

**BLACK NANCY DREW.** To get to the other genocide.

**BECCA.** That's not funny.

   That's offensive.

**BLACK NANCY DREW.** Debbie Downer.

**BECCA.** Negative Nancy.

**BLACK NANCY DREW.** Doggonit, for the love of Mike, will you get off your high horse?

**PONY.** *Pardonez moi?*

   Did someone say horse?

                    (*The* **PONY** *has entered.*)

*[MUSIC NO. 6: "PONIES"]*

**PONY.**

> PONIES DON'T LIKE TO HAVE GIRLFRIENDS
> SO PLEASE STOP ASKING
> PONIES
> PONIES
> DON'T WANT TO GO STEADY
> WE'RE JUST NOT READY
> PONIES
>
> YOU LOOK SO BEAUTIFUL TODAY
> HAVE YOU DONE SOMETHING DIFF'RENT WITH YOUR HAIR?
> I DIDN'T CALL YOU LAST NIGHT CUZ IT NEVER CROSSED MY
>   MIND.
> I'M A PONY.
> I'M JUST A PONY.
> AND THE ONLY WORDS I KNOW ARE:
>
> HUBBA HUBBA:
> THAT MEANS "I LIKE YOU."
> HUBBA HUBBA:
> "CAN I HAVE AN APPLE? PLEASE?"
> HUBBA HUBBA:
> "I DON'T TRUST HUMANS."
> HUBBA HUBBA:
> "I'M SORRY IF YOU THINK I'M MEAN."
>
> YOU LOOK SO BEAUTIFUL TODAY
> HAVE YOU ALWAYS BEEN SO THIN?
> I DIDN'T CALL YOU LAST NIGHT
> CUZ I JUST WENT STRAIGHT TO BED.
>
> I'M A PONY.
> I'M JUST A PONY.
> AND THAT'S JUST HOW PONIES ARE.
>
> PONIES DON'T WANNA HAVE GIRLFRIENDS.
> DON'T WANNA GO STEADY.
> PONIES.

> *(The* **PONY** *exits.)*

(**AMANDA** *runs on stage.*)

**AMANDA.** Ouch!

**BECCA.** What's wrong?

**AMANDA.** The cheerleaders are after me!

They all have diarrhea.

**BECCA.** Why?

**AMANDA.** Because of the hay!

This is all your fault.

**BECCA.** Sorry.

**AMANDA.** It's not OK.

You ruin everything.

**BLACK NANCY DREW.** Need a lift?

**AMANDA.** Nancy Drew?

You're black?

**BLACK NANCY DREW.** I got a makeover.

See my boobs.

**AMANDA.** Cool.

I want a makeover.

I'm Amanda.

**BLACK NANCY DREW.** No foolin'.

She says you never talk to her.

**AMANDA.** Who?

**BLACK NANCY DREW.** Bookah.

**AMANDA.** I'm speechless.

**BLACK NANCY DREW.** Also, she's a racist.

**BECCA.** I swear I'm not a racist.

**AMANDA.** Prove it.

**BECCA.** Oh my God.

I'm, like, the least racist person in the whole, entire
school.

**AMANDA.** What'd you do?

Take a poll?

Nice.

**BLACK NANCY DREW.** Right?

**BECCA.** I didn't take a poll.

**AMANDA.** Defensive much?

**BLACK NANCY DREW.** Offensive much?

**BECCA.** Me?

Offensive?

That's the pot calling the kettle –

**BLACK NANCY DREW.** Black?

**BECCA.** I didn't say that.

**BLACK NANCY DREW.** Maybe you didn't say it but you *thought* it.

**BECCA.** No I didn't!

You don't know anything!

**BLACK NANCY DREW.** I know you're homophobic.

**BECCA.** I'm so not homophobic!

**AMANDA.** A homophobic lesbian?

That's ironic.

**BLACK NANCY DREW.** What's ironic?

**AMANDA.** It's a three syllable word beginning with I.

Of all letters.

Much like Ohio.

*(***MR. HILL*** enters.)*

**MR. HILL.** Iowa!

I'm back.

Stupid creditors.

**BLACK NANCY DREW.** Where to, Mr. Hill?

**MR. HILL.** Do you have a map?

I'm lost in your eyes.

**AMANDA.** *(with flourish)* Auschwitz!

To Auschwitz!

**BLACK NANCY DREW.** So long, Burqa!

Good luck changing the world!

One poem at a time!

**MR. HILL.** Shotgun.

**BLACK NANCY DREW.** Rascal.

    *(**MR. HILL** exits.)*

**AMANDA.** Are you wearing lipstick?

**BECCA.** Tinted chapstick.

**AMANDA.** Take it off.

    You look like a skank!

**BECCA.** That's the pot calling the kettle African American.

    Snap!

**BLACK NANCY DREW.** Amanda.

    Quick question.

    Can I have the name of your therapist?

**AMANDA.** Sandy.

**BLACK NANCY DREW.** Like the hurricane?

**AMANDA.** Like the dog.

**BLACK NANCY DREW.** Thanks.

**AMANDA.** You OK?

**BLACK NANCY DREW.** I'm OK.

**AMANDA.** I come from a broken home.

**BLACK NANCY DREW.** I need someone to talk to about race.

    And fame.

    Celebrity's a bee-yotch.

    And Ned won't leave me alone.

**AMANDA.** Nancy.

    We should go.

**BECCA.** Can I tag along?

**AMANDA.** Paparazzi.

**PAPARAZZI.**

    Nancy, over here!

    You look beautiful!

    How's your day?

    Nancy, how's Ned?

    Did you really dance at the country club?

    Nancy, who are you wearing?

Is it true about the haunted bridge?
Is it true about the Swedish diary?
Is it true about the moss-covered mansion?

**BLACK NANCY DREW.** No comment!
I said no comment!

Simmer down!
Button up!
Zip it!
You stupid nosebleed!
Can it!
You dumb mug!

Shut your pie hole!
Shut your trap!

Back up!
You're blocking my roadster!
Back the frig up!
Get your mitts off my pencil skirt!

**CHILD.** Can I have your autograph?

**BLACK NANCY DREW.** Scram!
I said scram!
Anklebiter!

>           *(They exit.)*

>           *(**BECCA** is alone.)*

>           *(The **PONY** enters.)*

>           *(Slow, spacious music underneath.)*

**PONY.** Hi.

**BECCA.** Sorry, what?

**PONY.** I said hi.

**BECCA.** Oh, hi.

**PONY.** Tell me something.

**BECCA.** Sure.

**PONY.** How does it feel to be prettiest girl in the room?

BECCA. Who me?

(*The* **CHEERLEADER** *enters.*)

**CHEERLEADER.** Outta my way.

BECCA. The prettiest girl in the room?

Do you mean it?

PONY. (*looking at the* **CHEERLEADER**) Never mind.

Hey there.

**CHEERLEADER.** Hey.

BECCA. I don't think of myself as pretty.

More like girl-next-door-ish.

I'm probably a five or a six.

Maybe a seven.

On a good day.

I'm short.

And my ears stick out.

I heard about some procedure where they staple back your ears.

Probably costs a fortune.

I don't know.

Should I save up?

Or stick it out.

Get it?

That was a joke.

(**PONY** *and* **CHEERLEADER** *have fallen asleep.*)

(*They snore.*)

(**BECCA** *approaches the audience.*)

*[MUSIC NO. 7: "PSST I'M A POET"]*

**BECCA.**

PSST I'M A POET
I'VE ALWAYS BEEN.

I'VE ALWAYS BEEN A RHYMER
A ONCE UPON A TIMER.

SINCE I WAS TWO

OR THREE.
I'D WRITE POEM AFTER POEM
BUT I'D NEVER, EVER SHOW 'EM
TO ANYONE
'TIL NOW

Wanna see?
IT CAN BE OUR SECRET
I HOPE THAT YOU CAN KEEP IT
BETWEEN YOU AND ME
WHEE...
SORRY TO BE CHEESY
BUT RHYMES COME EASY
TO ME
LOOK AND SEE
ME
I'VE ALWAYS BEEN –

*[MUSIC NO 8: "FUN!"]*

SANDY.

> I'VE ALWAYS BEEN THE CORK
> STUCK IN THE BOTTLE OF SOME AWFUL CHEAP CHAMPAGNE
> LEFT ALONE INSIDE A DUSTY BOX
> AND NEVER OPENED CUZ THE PARTY'S OVER
> THE PARTY'S LONG BEEN OVER
>
> THERE'S A DRINKER SOMEWHERE, ISN'T THERE?
> TO DIG HIS THUMBS IN ME AND POP ME FREE?
> OH I'VE ALWAYS BEEN THE CORK STUCK IN THE BOTTLE.
>
> BUT THEN YOU SHOOK ME UP
> YOU SHOOK ME
> YOU SHOOK ME
> YOU SHOOK ME UP
> YOU SHOOK ME 'TIL I POPPED
> AND FLEW ACROSS THE ROOM! JUST A LIKE A PLANE!
> AND HOLY GOD!
> IS THERE ANYTHING IN ALL CREATION MORE DELICIOUS
> THAN A GLASS OF CHEAP CHAMPAGNE?
>
> MAMA'S TIPSY.
> FUN!
> MAMA'S TIPSY.
> FUN!
> MAMA'S TIPSY.
> FUN!
> MAMA'S ABOUT TO GET NAKED.
> FUN!
> I'M MORE BEAUTIFUL THAN I WAS WHEN I WAS SEVENTEEN!

LIZ, CHILD, AMANDA, NANCY DREW.

> YOU LOOK YOUNGER.

| SANDY. | LIZ, CHILD, AMANDA, NANCY DREW |
|---|---|
| MAMA'S TIPSY. | OOH |
| FUN! | FUN! |
| MAMA'S TIPSY. | OOH |
| FUN! | FUN! |
| MAMA'S TIPSY. | OOH |
| FUN! | FUN! |

**SANDY, LIZ, CHILD, AMANDA, NANCY DREW.**
> MAMA'S ON HER SECOND BOTTLE.
> WHEE!

**SANDY.**
> I'M MORE BEAUTIFUL THAN ANYONE.

**COMPANY.**
> YOU'RE TERRIFIC.

**SANDY, LIZ, CHILD, AMANDA, NANCY DREW.**
> FREE FREE FREE FREE FREE FREE FREE FREE

**SANDY.** I can set the house on fire if I wanna!

**LIZ, CHILD, AMANDA, NANCY DREW.**
> I THINK YOU WANNA!

**SANDY, LIZ, CHILD, AMANDA, NANCY DREW.**
> FREE FREE FREE FREE FREE FREE FREE FREE.

**SANDY.** All this champagne could put fire out!

**LIZ, CHILD, AMANDA, NANCY DREW.**
> DRINK MORE.
> POUR IT OVER EVERYTHING AND YOU'RE

| **SANDY.** | **LIZ, CHILD, AMANDA, NANCY DREW.** |
|---|---|
| MAMA'S SIPSY | FREE |
| FUN! | FUN! |
| | SO COOL! |

**SANDY.**
> MAMA SHAVED EV'RY HAIR

**AMANDA.** Gross.

**SANDY.**
> I'M MORE FLEXIBLE THAN ANYONE.

**COMPANY.**
> YOU'RE SO BENDY.

**SANDY, LIZ, CHILD, AMANDA, NANCY DREW.**
> BUBBLY BUBBLY BUBBLY BUBBLY

**SANDY.** Bubbly bubbly bubbly bubbly bubbly bubbly bubbly bubbly

**COMPANY.**
> YOU CAN DO BETTER.

**COMPANY.**

    BUBBLY BUBBLY BUBBLY BUBBLY

    DRINK MORE!

    POUR IT OVER EVERYTHING AND YOU'RE

| **SANDY.** | **COMPANY.** |
|---|---|
| MAMA'S BUBB'LY | FREE |
| FUN! | FUN! |
| MAMA'S BLUBBLY! COOL! | SO COOL! |

**SANDY.**

    BUBBLY MAMA! WHEE!

    MAMA'S ABOUT TO GET NASTY

**LIZ, CHILD, AMANDA, NANCY DREW.**

    WE'LL HELP!

    YOU'RE GODDAMN BEAUTIFUL

    YES YOU ARE, WHAT ARE YOU, SEVENTEEN

**SANDY.**

    I LOOK YOUNGER

**SANDY, LIZ, CHILD, AMANDA, NANCY DREW.**

    MAMA'S TIPSY

    MAMA'S TIPSY

    MAMA'S TIPSY

| **COMPANY.** | **SANDY.** |
|---|---|
| SHE'S MORE INTERESTING THAN ANYONE! | I'm interesting. |
| SHE'S MORE BEAUTIFUL THAN ANYONE! | I'm beautiful. |
| SHE'S MORE BUBBILY THAN ANYONE! | I'm bubbly. |

**SANDY.**

    I'M NOT DRUNK JUST

    TIPSY.

(**SANDY** *and* **BECCA** *drive.*)

(**PONY** *and* **CHEERLEADER** *wake up.*)

(*Slow, spacious.*)

**PONY.** Morning, Genius.

**CHEERLEADER.** Morning.

Where am I?

Who are you?

What time is it?

Where's my phone?

I have to call my stepmom.

Wait a minute.

Did I have sex with a pony?

**PONY.** You know it.

**CHEERLEADER.** You used a condom, right?

You used a condom.

You used a condom, right?

Tell me you used a condom.

Oh my God.

You didn't use a condom.

**PONY.** Sorry, Genius.

They don't make 'em in my size.

**CHEERLEADER.** Where's my lip balm?

Found it.

Text me, OK?

Or gimme a call.

**PONY.** Are you in the book?

**CHEERLEADER.** What's *the book*?

### [MUSIC NO. 9: "I DON'T KNOW"]

**SANDY.**

> I DON'T KNOW HOW THE CAR WORKS.
> AND I DON'T KNOW WHERE THE GAS GOES.
> AND I DON'T KNOW WHAT HEADLIGHTS DO.
> BUT I KNOW WHO DOES.
> YOU.

**PONY.** *(to the audience)* Merry Christmas.

| **SANDY.** | **BECCA.** |
|---|---|
| I | YOU GOTTA LEARN A THING OR TWO I TELL YA WHAT WOULD |
| DON'T KNOW | YOU DO WITHOUT ME? WHERE WOULD YOU BE? |
| WHAT THAT SIGN SAYS 'CAUSE I | |
| | YOU'D HIT A POLE OR TAKE A TURN AND END UP IN |
| DON'T KNOW HOW TO READ! Don't tell what's his name. | TIMBUKTU WITHOUT ME |

**SANDY & BECCA.**

> OH I DON'T KNOW WHAT

**SANDY.**

> "SENTENCES" DO
> BUT I KNOW WHO DOES:

**BECCA.**

> WHO?

**SANDY.**

> YOU
> DO EV'RYTHING FOR ME.

| **SANDY.** | **BECCA.** |
|---|---|
| I DON'T KNOW | DA-DA DUP DA-DA DUP DA DA DA DA DA DA DA DA DUP DA DA DA DUP |
| WHERE MY PURSE IS AND I | |
| | DA-DA DUP DA-DA DUP |

                                    DA DA DUP
    DON'T KNOW                DA DA
    WHY YOU'RE CRYING

**CHEERLEADER.** Where's my purse?

**SANDY.**

    AND I DON'T KNOW WHAT I'M S'POSED TO DO.

    BUT I KNOW WHO DOES:

**BECCA.**

    YOU KNOW WHO DOES

**SANDY.**

    I KNOW WHO DOES: YOU.

**CHEERLEADER.** *(texting)* Dear Pony,
    I have herpes.
    You know what?
    Delete.
    Dear Pony,
    Last night was super fun.
    xoxo,
    Jessica.
    Delete.
    Jess.

# PART III

## IOWA

(**SANDY** *and* **BECCA** *have arrived at* **ROGER**'*s home in Iowa.*)

(**SANDY** *rings the door bell.*)

(*They wait.*)

**SANDY.** It smells like cow poo.

**BECCA.** I guess that makes sense considering we're on a farm.

**SANDY.** Funny, Roger never mentioned he was a farmer.
Curve ball.
Farmers are a dying breed.
With negative income.
NBD.
Lesson four hundred and seven.
If life throws you a curve ball, knock it out of the park.
That's a metaphor.
For baseball.  ·
Our national pastime.

**BECCA.** What are you doing?

**SANDY.** Sexting Jesus.
He wants another picture of my boob.
Click.
Ask and ye shall receive.

> (*texting*)

Here's a picture of my boob and also Becca slightly smiling.
There's a first.
Send.
You should really smile more.
Braces aren't forever.

**BECCA.** I don't have braces.

**SANDY.** Open wide.

If I were you, I'd consider getting braces.

Your smile is your greatest asset.

It's the first thing people see.

Before your eyes.

Or even your boobs.

Lesson four hundred and eight.

One boob is always bigger than the other.

**BECCA.** I know.

**SANDY.** How do you know?

**BECCA.** School.

**SANDY.** Do you go to porn school?

*(**ROGER** opens the door.)*

*(He is surrounded by his wives and children.)*

**ROGER.** Sandy!

Hello!

**SANDY.** Roger!

Click!

Where's my engagement ring?

Confession:

I have herpes and my heart belongs to Jesus.

**ROGER.** Welcome to Iowa!

How do you like it?

**SANDY.** Dear Diary,

I'm confused.

*(**ROGER** vomits on **SANDY**'s shoes.)*

My shoes!

**WIFE 1 / LIZ.** Children come quick.

Daddy barfed all over new Mommy's shoes.

**WIFE 2 / CHEERLEADER.** Daddy's gag reflex is super, super
sensitive.

**WIFE 3 / AMANDA.** Daddy can't help it that he barfs at the drop of a hat.

> *(Someone drops a hat.)*

> *(**ROGER** barfs again.)*

**WIFE 4 / NANCY DREW.** Plus he's been hitting the sauce again.

**ROGER.** No I haven't.

**WIFE 4 / NANCY DREW.** Yes you have.

**ROGER.** I was celebrating!

**SANDY.** Who are all these children?
I'm counting more than six.

**ROGER.** I have sixty.

**SANDY.** You have sixteen?

**ROGER.** I have six oh.

**SANDY.** You have one six?

**WIFE 1 / LIZ.** He has sixty.

**BECCA.** Sixty-one.

**SANDY.** Seventeen?

**ROGER.** And counting!

> *(**ROGER** passes out.)*

**WIFE 2 / CHEERLEADER.** Someone give Daddy a cold shower.

**SANDY.** Who are you?

> *(Piano begins.)*

**WIFE 3 / AMANDA.** So, I'm Karyn.

**WIFE 1 / LIZ.** And I'm April.

**WIFE 4 / NANCY DREW.** And I'm Cindy.

**WIFE 2 / CHEERLEADER.** And I'm Lisa.

**WIFE 4 / NANCY DREW.** And I'm Annie.

**WIFE 3 / AMANDA.** And I'm Lori.

**WIFE 2 / CHEERLEADER.** And I'm Kolette.

**WIFE 1 / LIZ.** And I'm Jill.

**WIVES.**
WELCOME, WELCOME

**SANDY.** Funny, Roger never mentioned he was a polygamist.
Red flag.

Are polygamists people too?

Any thoughts, D?

**WIFE 3 / AMANDA.** He has it on his Facebook page.

**WIFE 4 / NANCY DREW.** Under basic info.

**WIFE 1 / LIZ.** I don't know how you missed it.

Anyway –

**ALL WIVES.**

WELCOME, WELCOME!

**WIFE 2 / CHEERLEADER.** Where's your luggage?

**SANDY.** The cloud.

Everything we own is in the cloud.

And it's wonderful.

To feel so free.

Unencumbered.

Hallelujah!

Jesus sexted me back.

He has man boobs.

Have a look.

**WIFE 3 / AMANDA.** Roger showed us your Facebook profile,
and we agreed you looked perfect.

**SANDY.** Perfect?

**WIFE 4 / NANCY DREW.** Exactly the kind of wife we need to
make our family whole.

**WIFE 1 / LIZ.** Educated, cosmopolitan, great sense of humor.

**SANDY.** *(modest)* Stop…

**WIFE 2 / CHEERLEADER.** Successful, independent, terrific
sense of style.

**SANDY.** Go on…

**WIFE 1 / LIZ.** Who cares about a little credit card debt.

**WIFE 4 / NANCY DREW.** We all have our flaws.

**WIFE 3 / AMANDA.** Like Samantha here.

She's a total slob.

Never flushes the toilet.

**WIFE 2 / CHEERLEADER**. Well, at least I'm not a mouth breather like you, Sarah B.

**WIFE 4 / NANCY DREW**. It's true, Sarah B.
You breathe like a rhino.

**WIFE 3 / AMANDA**. It's not my fault I have asthma.

**WIFE 1 / LIZ**. You look like a rhino.

**WIFE 4 / NANCY DREW**. I have an issue with my thyroid.

**WIFE 2 / CHEERLEADER**. I have an issue with my mother-in-law.

**WIFE 3 / AMANDA**. I have an issue with my GI tract.
I keep having ulcerations.

**WIFE 1 / LIZ**. I keep having altercations.

**WIFE 4 / NANCY DREW**. I keep having palpitations.

**WIFE 2 / CHEERLEADER**. I keep having fluctuations.

**SANDY**. Hey, where are you going?

**ALL WIVES**. Caroling!

**WIFE 1 / LIZ**. We're going caroling.

**WIFE 3 / AMANDA**. This year, we're going caroling.

**WIFE 2 / CHEERLEADER**. We always say we're going caroling, but we never go.

**ALL WIVES**. Come with?

**BECCA**. No thanks.

**SANDY**. Mind your manners, Bookah.

**WIFE 1 / LIZ**. Bookah?
Who's Bookah?

**SANDY**. My adopted, lesbian, racist daughter.
Not to name names.
She doesn't like the Jews.
Plus she's homophobic.
How's that for oxymoronic?
Are you familiar with oxymoronic?
It's a five syllable word beginning with O.
Of all letters.
Much like Iowa.

**ROGER.** Ohio.

**SANDY.** Burqa's saving the world.

One poem at a time.

**WIFE 3 / AMANDA.** A poet?

**WIFE 2 / CHEERLEADER.** She's a poet?

**WIFE 1 / LIZ.** You're a poet?

**WIFE 4 / NANCY DREW.** Burqa's a poet?

**WIFE 3 / AMANDA.** I can't believe you're poet.

Poetry is my passion.

**WIFE 2 / CHEERLEADER.** Poetry is my escape.

**WIFE 1 / LIZ.** Poetry is my thing.

**WIFE 4 / NANCY DREW.** Recite us one of your poems.

**WIFE 3 / AMANDA.** We'd love to hear a poem.

**WIFE 2 / CHEERLEADER.** I can't wait to hear a poem!

**WIFE 1 / LIZ.** Please.

**WIFE 4 / NANCY DREW.** Share a poem!

**ALL WIVES.** POEM POEM!

**SANDY.** Go on.

Don't be shy.

*[MUSIC NO. 10: "PSST I'M NOT A POET"]"*

**BECCA.** .

PSST I'M NOT A POET.
I'VE NEVER BEEN.
WELL, I WROTE A CRAPPY POEM WHEN I WAS TEN.
MY POEMS WERE BETTER THOUGH STILL NOT GREAT.
JUST A LOT LESS CRAPPY WHEN I WAS EIGHT.
IF TIME WENT BACKWARDS, I THINK WE'D SEE,
I WAS THE BEST POET I'D EVER BE
WHEN I WAS THREE.
I WROTE A POEM INSIDE MY MOM.
BUT I FORGET.
WELL, MOVING ON.
I'M FOURTEEN AND IT'S TIME
AND THAT'S MY FINAL RHYME!
POETIC IS PATHETIC
BLOW ME!
NEVER MIND

Suck it!

(*The* **WIVES** *and* **SANDY** *boo.*)

**SANDY.** Where are you going?

**BECCA.** For a walk.

**WIFE 1 / LIZ.** Take a flashlight.

**BECCA.** OK.

**SANDY.** She has an issue with her attitude.
It's hormone-related.

*[MUSIC NO. 11: "ORATORIO"]*

**WIFE 1 / LIZ.**

    I HAVE AN ISSUE WITH MY BACK.
    IT'S ANXIETY RELATED.

**WIFE 2 / CHEERLEADER.**

    I HAVE AN ISSUE WITH MY CAR.
    IT'S TEMPERATURE RELATED.

**WIFE 4 / NANCY DREW.**

    I KEEP HAVING FLARE UPS.

**WIFE 1 / LIZ.**

    I KEEP HAVING NOSEBLEEDS.

**WIFE 2 / CHEERLEADER.**

    I KEEP HAVING MELTDOWNS.

**WIFE 3 / AMANDA.**

    I KEEP HAVING PANIC DREAMS.

**WIFE 4 / NANCY DREW.**

    SHUT UP, SARAH B.

**WIFE 3 / AMANDA.**

    QUIT CALLING ME SARAH B.
    CAN'T I BE JUST SARAH FOR ONCE?

**WIFE 1 / LIZ.**

    CAN'T I JUST BE HAPPY FOR ONCE?

**WIFE 2 / CHEERLEADER.**

    CAN'T I JUST BE RIGHT FOR ONCE?

| **WIFE 1 / LIZ.** | **WIFE 4 / NANCY DREW.** | **WIFE 3 / AMANDA.** |
|---|---|---|
| CAN'T I JUST BE | ENOUGH WITH | |
| NORMAL FOR | THE INCESSANT | |
| ONCE ENOUGH | WHINING ENOUGH | ENOUGH WITH |
| WITH THE | WITH THE IN- | THE INCESSANT |
| INCESSANT | -CESSANT NITPI- | POPUP ADS |
| TAPPING OH | CKING, TAPPING, | CAN'T I JUST |
| CAN'T I JUST BE | WHINING AND | BE HAPPY |
| ENOUGH WITH | QUIT CALLING | SARAH |
| THE WHINING | ME SARAH B. | CAN'T I BE? |

**WIFE 2 / CHEERLEADER.** *(overlapping with above:)*

    CAN'T I JUST BE RIGHT FOR ONCE?
    CAN'T I JUST BE RIGHT FOR ONCE?

CAN'T I JUST BE RIGHT FOR ONCE?

**WIFE 1 / LIZ.**

WHY CAN'T YOU WEAR A BRA FOR ONCE?

I'M SO SICK OF YOUR POINTY NIPPLES I COULD SCREAM.

| **WIFE 2 / CHEERLEADER.** | **OTHER WIVES.** |
| --- | --- |
| I'M SO SICK OF YOUR | GRR... |
| VICTIM MENTALITY | |

**WIFE 4 / NANCY DREW.**

| I'M SO SICK OF YOUR | GRR... |
| --- | --- |
| FLORAL HEADBANDS | |

**WIFE 1 / LIZ.**

| I'M SO SICK OF YOUR | GRR... |
| --- | --- |
| UNGRATEFUL ASS | |

**WIFE 3 / AMANDA.**

| I'M SO SICK OF YOUR | GRR... |
| --- | --- |
| HOLIER-THAN-THOU ATTITUDE | |

**WIFE 4 / NANCY DREW.** I'm so sick of your god-damned kids.

**WIFE 1 / LIZ.** I'm so sick of your god-damned lies, you two-faced bitch.

**WIFE 2 / CHEERLEADER.**

MERRY CHRISTMAS, CAROLINE.

**WIFE 1 / LIZ.**

MY NAME'S CAROLYN.

| **WIFE 3 / AMANDA.** | **OTHER WIVES.** |
| --- | --- |
| I'M YOUR SECRET SANTA, | MERRY |
| AND I'M GIVING YOU COAL | CHRISTMAS |

**WIFE 4 / NANCY DREW.**

| I'M YOUR SECRET SANTA, | HARK HOW |
| --- | --- |
| AND I'M GIVING YOU BOOGERS | THE BELLS |

**WIFE 1 / LIZ.**

| I'M YOUR SECRET SANTA | JESUS |
| --- | --- |
| AND I'M GIVING YOU BONES | CHRIST |

**SANDY.** Jesus' bones?

| **WIFE 2 / CHEERLEADER.** | **OTHER WIVES.** |
| --- | --- |
| YOU JUST RUINED SECRET SANTA | HA HA HA HA |

**WIVES 1 & 2.**

| I HOPE YOU'RE HAPPY! | HA HA HA HA HAPPY? |
| --- | --- |

**WIFE 3 / AMANDA.**

WELL, YOU RUINED MY DISNEYLAND AUTOGRAPH BOOK SO
WE'RE EVEN.

**ALL WIVES.**

CHRISTMAS!

**WIFE 2 / CHEERLEADER.**

I HATE SECRET SANTA.

YEAH.

**WIFE 1 / LIZ.**

SECRET SANTA SUCKS.

| **WIFE 4 / NANCY DREW.** | **OTHER WIVES.** |
|---|---|
| THANKS FOR THE STARBUCKS GIFT CARD EVEN THOUGH I DON'T DRINK COFFEE! | RRUM RRUM RRUM PUM PUM RRUM PUM PUM PUM |

**WIFE 1 / LIZ.** Since when?

**WIFE 3 / AMANDA.**

COFFEE HAS ANTIOXIDANTS.

**WIFE 1 / LIZ.**

YOU COULD HAVE SAID THAT IN A NICER TONE.

| **WIFE 2/ CHEERLEADER.** | **OTHER WIVES.** |
|---|---|
| MAYBE IF YOU DIDN'T COMPLAIN ALL DAY PEOPLE WOULD TAKE YOU SERIOUSLY | RRUM RRUM RRUM PUM PUM RRUM PUM PUM PUM |

| **WIFE 4 / NANCY DREW.** | |
|---|---|
| MAYBE PEOPLE WOULD TAKE YOU SERIOUSLY IF YOU WEREN'T SUCH A TOTAL IDIOT! | RRUM RRUM RRUM PUM PUM RRUM PUM PUM PUM ANTIOXIDANT! |

**WIFE 1 / LIZ.**

I HAVEN'T BEEN HAPPY IN YEARS.

**WIFE 4 / NANCY DREW.**

I'M JUST GOING THROUGH THE MOTIONS.

**WIFE 2 / CHEERLEADER.**

I'M LIVING HALF A LIFE.

**WIFE 3 / AMANDA.**

I FEEL TRAPPED IN MY LIFE, AND I HATE IT.

**WIFE 1 / LIZ.**

I FEEL TRAPPED IN MY JOB.

**WIFE 4 / NANCY DREW.**

I FEEL TRAPPED IN MY HEAD.

**WIFE 3 / AMANDA.**

I FEEL TRAPPED IN THIS HOUSE.

**WIFE 2 / CHEERLEADER.**

I FEEL TRAPPED IN THE WORLD.

| **WIFE 1 / LIZ.** | **WIFE 4 / NANCY DREW.** |
|---|---|
| WHY DO I FEEL TRAPPED | WHY… |
| IN MY BODY? | **WIVES 2 & 3** |
| I'M JUST A | WHY |
| | **WIVES 2, 3 & 4** |
| POUND OVER MY IDEAL WEIGHT | WHY |
| THAT SAID | |

**WIFE 2 / CHEERLEADER.**

I HAVE GAS PAINS.

**WIFE 1 / LIZ.**

MY

**WIFE 4 / NANCY DREW.**

MY FEET HURT.

**WIFE 1 / LIZ.**

KNEES

**WIFE 3 / AMANDA.**

GOODBYE.

**WIFE 1 / LIZ.**

HURT

**WIFE 3 / AMANDA.**

GOODBYE.

**WIFE 1 / LIZ.**

WHERE ARE YOU GOING?

**WIFE 3 / AMANDA.**

TO KILL MYSELF.

**WIFE 2 / CHEERLEADER.**

NOT AGAIN.

**WIFE 4 / NANCY DREW.**

I WISH YOU WOULD STOP SAYING YOU'RE GONNA KILL
YOURSELF AND JUST DO IT ALREADY?

YOU'VE MADE THESE PAST FIFTEEN YEARS A LIVING HELL
FOR US.

**WIFE 1 / LIZ.**

YOU'VE MADE THESE PAST SIX MONTHS COMPLETELY
WORTHWHILE.
HONESTLY, I COULDN'T HAVE ASKED FOR A BETTER GROUP
OF GUYS.

**WIFE 3 / AMANDA.**

I COULDN'T HAVE ASKED FOR A WARMER WELCOME.

**WIFE 4 / NANCY DREW.**

I COULDN'T HAVE ASKED FOR A BETTER OUTCOME.

**ALL WIVES.**

EVEN THOUGH GETTING HERE WAS HELL.

**WIFE 3 / AMANDA.**

YOU'VE MADE THESE PAST THREE YEARS

**ALL WIVES.**

YOU'VE MADE THESE PAST THREE YEARS
YOU'VE MADE THESE PAST THREE YEARS A GREAT EXPERIENCE.
YOU RULE!
OH!
YOU'VE MADE THESE PAST TWENTY MONTHS FEEL LIKE
TWENTY MINUTES.
STAY GOLD!
OH!

**WIFE 1 / LIZ.**

YOU'VE MADE THESE PAST EIGHT MONTHS INTERESTING.
IN A GOOD WAY THOUGH.
MOSTLY.

**ALL WIVES.**

WHAT A RIDE!
EVEN THOUGH GETTING HERE WAS HELL.

**WIFE 1 / LIZ.**

I WASN'T RAISED TO BELIEVE IN HELL.

**WIFE 4 / NANCY DREW.**

I WASN'T RAISED IN YOUR STRATOSPHERE.

**WIFE 3 / AMANDA.**

I WASN'T RAISED TO BE BILINGUAL.
WHICH HAS ALWAYS KIND OF BUMMED ME OUT.

**WIFE 2 / CHEERLEADER.**

HEROES.

I DON'T HAVE ANY.

WHICH HAS ALWAYS KIND OF BUMMED ME OUT.

**WIFE 1 / LIZ.**

I WASN'T RAISED TO BELIEVE IN TRUE LOVE.

**WIVES 2, 3 & 4.**

TRUE LOVE!

**WIFE 1 / LIZ.** But somehow I became a hopeless romantic.

**WIFE 4 / NANCY DREW.**

WOULD YOU PLEASE STOP TALKING ABOUT MY CAREER IN
THE PAST TENSE?

**WIFE 3 / AMANDA.**

WOULD YOU PLEASE STOP TALKING ABOUT MY
REPRODUCTIVE ORGANS?

**WIFE 1 / LIZ.**

WOULD YOU PLEASE STOP DELUDING YOURSELF?

**WIFE 2 / CHEERLEADER.**

WOULD YOU PLEASE STOP SENDING ME E-CARDS?

**WIFE 4 / NANCY DREW.**

WOULD YOU PLEASE STOP IGNORING ME BECAUSE IT'S
SENDING ME INTO DESPAIR.

**WIFE 1 / LIZ.**

BECAUSE IT'S SENDING ME INTO A TAIL-

| **WIFE 1 / LIZ.** | **WIFE 3 / AMANDA.** | **WIVES 2 & 3.** |
|---|---|---|
| -SPIN | BECAUSE IT'S | BECAUSE IT'S |

**ALL WIVES.**

SENDING ME

**WIVES 2 & 3.**

INTO WITHDRAWAL.

**WIVES 1 & 4.**

INTO OVERDRIVE.

**WIFE 1 / LIZ.**

BECAUSE IT'S SENDING ME INTO NEW TERRITORY.

**WIFE 4 / NANCY DREW.**

WOULD YOU PLEASE STOP SPITTING WHEN YOU TALK?

**WIFE 2 / CHEERLEADER.**

WOULD YOU PLEASE STOP PUTTING YOUR COAT ON TOP OF MY COAT?

**WIFE 1 / LIZ.**

WOULD YOU PLEASE STOP DEFENDING ME?

I DON'T NEED DEFENDING.

**WIFE 2 / CHEERLEADER.**

I DO NOT NEED GOD.

**WIFE 3 / AMANDA.**

I DO NOT NEED ALL THIS INFORMATION.

**WIVES 1 & 2.**

I DO NOT NEED FITNESS EQUIPMENT.

**WIFE 3 / AMANDA.**

I DO NOT NEED A LAWYER.

DO I?

**WIFE 1 / LIZ.**

I DO NOT NEED ADDITIONAL TRAINING.

**WIFE 4 / NANCY DREW.**

I DO NOT NEED ALL THIS SHIT WHEN MY ACUPUNCTURIST IS OUT OF TOWN.

**ALL WIVES.**

I DO NOT NEED TO EXPLAIN WHY I SAY THINGS.

I DO NOT NEED TO EXPLAIN WHY I SAY THINGS.

I DO NOT NEED TO EXPLAIN WHY I SAY THINGS.

**WIFE 3 / AMANDA.**

THAT'S THE INTERESTING THING ABOUT BEING PRESIDENT.

**WIFE 4 / NANCY DREW.**

THAT'S THE INTERESTING THING ABOUT BEING A FATHER.

**WIFE 1 / LIZ.**

THAT'S THE INTERESTING THING ABOUT MY JOB.

I LIKE STRADDLING BOTH WORLDS.

**WIFE 2 / CHEERLEADER.**

I LIKE THE TASTE OF DOCTOR PEPPER.

**WIVES 1 & 3.**

THAT'S THE INTERESTING THING ABOUT DEFINING WHAT IS AND ISN'T PORN.

**WIFE 4 / NANCY DREW.**

I WASN'T RAISED TO BE ASHAMED OF MY BODY.

I'M JUST NATURALLY EXTREMELY MODEST.

**WIFE 1 / LIZ.**

I'M JUST NATURALLY EXTREMELY PALE.

**WIFE 2 / CHEERLEADER.**

I LIKE THE TASTE OF DR. PEPPER.

**WIFE 3 / AMANDA.**

I'M JUST NAT'RALLY EXTREMELY SHY.

**WIFE 2 / CHEERLEADER.**

I'M JUST NAT'RALLY EXTREMELY VOCAL.

**WIFE 1 / LIZ.**

I'M JUST NAT'RALLY EXTREMELY SENSITIVE.

TO MEDICATION.

**WIFE 4 / NANCY DREW.**

I'M JUST NAT'RALLY EXTREMELY SKEPTICAL OF OVER-HYPED
WEATHER EVENTS.

**WIFE 1 / LIZ.**

YOU HAVE TO UNDERSTAND I GREW UP IN A SMALL
WESTERN KANSAS TOWN.

| **WIFE 2 / CHEERLEADER.** | **WIVES 3 & 4.** |
|---|---|
| I grew up on the east side of St. Paul | I'M JUST NAT'RALLY EXTREMELY SHY |

| **WIFE 3 / AMANDA.** | **WIVES 1 & 4** |
|---|---|
| I grew up on the north end of Detroit | I'M JUST NAT'RALLY EXTREMELY VOCAL |

| **WIFE 4 / NANCY DREW.** | **WIVES 1 & 3.** |
|---|---|
| I grew up on the south end of Monroe. | I'M JUST NAT'RALLY EXTREMELY SENSITIVE |

**ALL WIVES.**

TO MEDICATION

| **WIFE 1 / LIZ.** | **OTHER WIVES.** |
|---|---|
| I grew up on the west side of Houston. | I'M JUST NAT'RALLY EXTR- -EMELY SKEPTICAL OF OV- |
| A pretty slow part of town. | -ERHYPED WEATHER EVENTS |

**ALL WIVES.**

I GREW UP ON THE PLAINS.

I GREW UP ON THE PRAIRIE.

I GREW UP ON THE OLSEN TWINS.

I GREW UP WITH HEAVY METAL.

I GREW UP WITH SCI-FI.

BECAUSE OF DAD.

**SANDY.** My dad?

I GREW UP...

**WIFE 1 / LIZ.** With a very woodsy kind of brother.

**WIFE 2 / CHEERLEADER.** Halfway around the world.

**WIFE 4 / NANCY DREW.** In a world that had Muppets but I was never really a Muppets person.

**WIFE 3 / AMANDA.** I was never really a people person.

**WIFE 1 / LIZ.** I was never really a glass half full kind of person.

**WIFE 4 / NANCY DREW.**

I GREW UP IN NEW YORK CITY.

HALF SOUTHERN.

HALF BROOKLYN.

**WIFE 3 / AMANDA.**

HALF NAVAJO.

HALF WHITE.

**WIFE 2 / CHEERLEADER.**

HALF A MILE DOWN THE ROAD.

**WIFE 4 / NANCY DREW.**

HALF WITH MOM.

HALF WITH DAD.

**WIFE 1 / LIZ.**

HALFWAY BETWEEN AGNOSTIC AND ATHEIST.

**WIFE 4 / NANCY DREW.**

HALFWAY BETWEEN THE COUNTRY AND CITY, HEY!

**ALL WIVES.**

HEY HEY HEY HEY HEY HEY HEY.

HEY HEY HEY HEY HEY HEY HEY.

**WIFE 1 / LIZ.**

SO I KINDA LOVE THEM BOTH.

**WIFE 4 / NANCY DREW.**

SO I KINDA LOVE TO COOK.

**WIFE 3 / AMANDA.**

SO I KINDA LOVE BAD MOVIES.

**WIFE 2 / CHEERLEADER.**

SO I KINDA LOVE THIS GUY AT WORK.

**WIFE 4 / NANCY DREW.**

SO I KINDA LOVE TO HATE STEVE JOBS.

**WIFE 1 / LIZ.**

I GREW UP HALF BELIEVING IN ASTROLOGY.

**WIFE 4 / NANCY DREW.**

I GREW UP HALF BELIEVING MY MOM DIDN'T DIE.

**ALL WIVES.**

HEY HEY HEY HEY HEY HEY HEY HEY.

HEY HEY HEY HEY HEY HEY HEY –

**WIFE 4 / NANCY DREW.**

I GUESS I THOUGHT SHE GOT MAD AND MOVED AWAY.

**ALL WIVES.**

HEY HEY HEY HEY HEY HEY HEY –

**WIFE 1 / LIZ.**

YOU HAVE TO UNDERSTAND, I GREW UP IN THE INNER CITY
OF PITTSBURGH.

ALL I EVER KNEW WAS THE STREETS.

**WIFE 2 / CHEERLEADER.**

ALL I EVER KNEW WAS HARD WORK.

**WIFE 4 / NANCY DREW.**

ALL I EVER KNEW WAS THE MILITARY.

**WIFE 3 / AMANDA.**

ALL I EVER KNEW WAS LOSING.

**WIFE 1 / LIZ.**

ALL I EVER KNEW WAS MONSTER TRUCKS.

**WIFE 2 / CHEERLEADER.**

ALL I EVER KNEW WAS THE CHORUS.

**WIFE 4 / NANCY DREW.**

ALL I EVER KNEW WAS 'OLD SCHOOL METHODS.'

**WIFE 1 / LIZ.**

ALL I EVER KNEW WAS MEAT AND POTATOES.

**WIFE 3 / AMANDA.**

    ALL I EVER KNEW WAS BOTTLING THINGS UP.

**WIFE 4 / NANCY DREW.**

    ALL I EVER KNEW WAS WE DIDN'T HAVE THE MONEY.

**ALL WIVES.**

    ALL I EVER KNEW WAS –

**WIFE 2 / CHEERLEADER.**

    OIL.

**WIFE 3 / AMANDA.**

    BANKING.

**WIFE 1 / LIZ.**

    HER FIRST NAME.

**WIFE 4 / NANCY DREW.**

    ALL I EVER KNEW WAS THAT HE HAD AN OFFICE
      DOWNTOWN.

**WIFE 3 / AMANDA.**

    ALL I EVER KNEW WAS POP-POP'S BROTHER HAD BEEN
      KILLED IN THE WAR.

**WIFE 1 / LIZ.**

    ALL I EVER KNEW WAS THE BLACK SIDE OF MY FAMILY.

**WIFE 4 / NANCY DREW.**

    ALL I EVER KNEW WAS ICEBERG LETTUCE.

**WIFE 1 / LIZ.**

    ALL I EVER KNEW WAS FAME.

**WIFE 4 / NANCY DREW.**

    AND DR. PEPPER.

**WIFE 2 / CHEERLEADER.**

    ALL I EVER KNEW WAS HE MOVED AWAY SUDDENLY.
    NO ONE TOLD ME WHY.
    I GUESS IT WAS JUST ONE OF THOSE THINGS.

**WIFE 3 / AMANDA.**

    ALL I EVER KNEW WAS I JUST HAD TO DO IT.

**ALL WIVES.**

    I JUST HAD TO GO FOR IT.
    I JUST HAD TO GIVE IT A TRY.
    I JUST HAD TO GIVE IT A SHOT.

NO MATTER WHAT THE ODDS.
NO MATTER WHAT THE PRICE.
NO MATTER WHAT THE OUTCOME.
NO MATTER WHAT THE COST.
ALL I EVER KNEW WAS THAT HE FELL OUT OF A TREE.
YOU HAVE TO UNDERSTAND, I GREW UP WHEN STUFF LIKE
    THIS WAS JUST COMING OUT.
MMMM...

*(Slow, spacious.)*

*(Filled with despair, longing, heartbreak.)*

**SANDY.** Dear Diary,

I don't know how to say this, but I think we need a break.

But I'm a little infatuated with you.

But I would love to spend the day with you.

The whole entire day with you.

I wish I could go back and spend the whole entire day with you.

Just you and me.

Watching movies.

On a Sunday.

We'll have a lazy day.

Let's have a lazy day.

You look beautiful all the time.

But I wish I could go back and pick your brain.

For half an hour.

And get inside your head.

But I wish I could go back and find you sooner.

Distraught face.

Quit Safari.

Screw the changes.

Don't save.

Shut down.

Beach ball, wait, spin, wait, spin, wait, slam, crash, explode.

Combust.

Into a million tiny pieces.

Into a million tiny shards.

Of flesh.

Of brain.

Microscopic.

Disintegrate.
Float away.

**ALL WIVES.**

    HEY HEY HEY HEY HEY HEY HEY

    HEY HEY HEY HEY HEY HEY HEY

    HEY HEY HEY HEY HEY HEY HEY

**WIFE 1 / LIZ.**

    YOU HAVE TO UNDERSTAND I'M DOING THIS BECAUSE OF

        LOVE, PEOPLE, LOVE!

**ALL WIVES.**

    I'M DOING THIS BECAUSE OF –

**WIFE 1 / LIZ.** High cholesterol!

**ALL WIVES.**

    I'M DOING THIS BECAUSE OF –

**WIFE 4 / NANCY DREW.** My third grade teacher!

**ALL WIVES.**

    I'M DOING THIS BECAUSE OF –

**WIFE 1 / LIZ.**

    TIME CONSTRAINTS! I DON'T HAVE TIME TO MESS AROUND!

**WIFE 3 / AMANDA.**

    I DON'T HAVE TIME TO READ BOOKS!

**WIFE 4 / NANCY DREW.**

    I DON'T HAVE TIME TO POST DAILY!

**WIFE 2 / CHEERLEADER.**

    I DON'T HAVE TIME TO PLAY GAMES.

**WIFE 1 / LIZ.**

You have to understand, I grew up on a farm with cherry and apple trees.

And they were beautiful in the spring.

**WIFE 4 / NANCY DREW.** And they were beautiful in the extreme.

**WIFE 3 / AMANDA.** And they were beautiful in the sense of earthly beauty.

**WIFE 2 / CHEERLEADER.** And they were beautiful in the sense that they really moved me.

**WIFE 1 / LIZ.** And they were beautiful in the prettiest shade of pink you ever saw.

**WIFE 4 / NANCY DREW.** And they were beautiful in the rear view mirror.

**WIFE 3 / AMANDA.** And they were beautiful in the eyes of the poet.

**WIFE 2 / CHEERLEADER.** And they were beautiful in the church on either side of the altar.

**WIFE 1 / LIZ.** And they were beautiful in the darkness, and he admired them.

**SANDY.** And they were beautiful in the sun, and I was happy.

**WIFE 1 / LIZ.** Here's your engagement ring.

**WIFE 3 / AMANDA.** Do you like it?

**SANDY.** I love it.

**WIFE 4 / NANCY DREW.** Let's show her to her wing.

**SANDY.** I have my own wing?!

**WIFE 2 / CHEERLEADER.** I'm blind.

**SANDY.** Do you speak English?

**WIFE 2 / CHEERLEADER.** I've always wanted to learn. Since I was a girl.

**SANDY.** *(coincidence) I* was a girl.

**WIFE 2 / CHEERLEADER.** Since I was a little girl.

**SANDY.** I'll teach you.

**WIFE 2 / CHEERLEADER.** You're a godsend.

**SANDY.** Actually, I'm a therapist.

**WIFE 1 / LIZ.** Say, do you like ponies?

**SANDY.** I love ponies.

*[MUSIC NO. 12: "IOWA"]*

**ROGER.**

I LIKE IOWA.

I LIKE IOWA.

I LIKE IOWA.

I – O – WA.

**ROGER, SISTER WIVES, SANDY.**

I LIKE IOWA.

I LIKE IOWA.

I LIKE IOWA.

I – O – WA.

**ROGER.** Well, this is Iowa.

**SISTER WIVES & SANDY.**

IOWA.

**ROGER.** Iowa.

**SISTER WIVES & SANDY.**

IOWA.

**ROGER.** I-o-wa…

Am I saying that wrong?

It sounds wrong:

**SISTER WIVES & SANDY.**

IOWA.

**ROGER.** Hmm.

There's commercial on the radio that says:

"I like Iowa."

**SISTER WIVES & SANDY.**

IOWA.

**ROGER.** "Come to Iowa."

**SISTER WIVES & SANDY.**

COME TO IOWA.

**COMPANY.**

I LIKE IOWA.

I LIKE IOWA.

I LIKE IOWA.

I-O-WA.

**ROGER.** You know I don't even remember how I got here.

**SISTER WIVES & SANDY.**

MMM...

**ROGER.** I just woke up one day

And I was a farmer in iowa.

**SISTER WIVES & SANDY.**

IOWAIOWAIOWAIOWAIOWA

**ROGER.** Isn't that funny?

**SISTER WIVES & SANDY.**

IOWAIOWAIOWAIOWAIOWAIOWAIOWAIOWAIOWAIOWAIOWA
IOWAIOWAIOWAIOWAIOWAIOWAIOWAIOWAIOWAIOWA
IOWAIOWA IOWAIOWAIOWAIOWAIOWAIOWAIOWAIOWA
IOWAIOWAIOWAIO WAIOWAIOWAIOWAIOWA

**ROGER.** Sorry

**SISTER WIVES & SANDY.**

MMM...

**ROGER.** I thought I had something to say,

But I don't.

**SISTER WIVES & SANDY.**

MMM...

**ROGER.** I just remember all these people saying,

"I like Iowa."

They never really said why.

"Come to Iowa."

"I'm pretty sure we're on the map."

> (**BECCA** *is left alone with a* **CHILD**.)

> (*They stare out at the horizon.*)

> (*Slow, spacious, forlorn, melancholy, distant, distracted, trapped.*)

**CHILD.** I'm leaving soon.

**BECCA.** Where are you going?

**CHILD.** Mars.

You don't believe me.

**BECCA.** I'm leaving too.

**CHILD.** Where are you going?

IOWA                    105

**BECCA.** That way.
**CHILD.** Which way?
**BECCA.** West.

> *(beat)*

**CHILD.** I'm Charlie.
**BECCA.** Hi, Charlie.
**CHILD.** Welcome to Iowa.
**BECCA.** Thanks.
**CHILD.** Do you miss your home?
**BECCA.** Not really.
**CHILD.** Do miss your friends?
**BECCA.** I don't have any friends.

> *(beat)*

Which one's your mom?
**CHILD.** The crazy one.
**BECCA.** You're funny.
For a little kid.
**CHILD.** I'm ten, actually.
**BECCA.** Double digits.
Congratulations.
**CHILD.** Thanks.

> *(beat)*

Will I be crazy?
When I grow up?
Will I be like…?
**BECCA.** Them?
No.
Of course not.
**CHILD.** Will it be sudden or gradual?
The process of going crazy?
**BECCA.** You're not gonna be crazy, Charlie.
**CHILD.** How do you know?
**BECCA.** I'm optimistic.

**CHILD.** I'm afraid.

>   *(beat)*

Will you send for me?

When you get settled?

**BECCA.** I'm not going anywhere.

I'm staying here with you.

**CHILD.** But what about the West?

**BECCA.** The West can wait.

>   *(beat)*

What should we do first?

**CHILD.** My hobbies are rocket building and bird watching.

I would like to get close to a *hawk*.

**BECCA.** Do you want to build a tree house?

**CHILD.** I already have a tree house.

**BECCA.** *(joking)* Sorry, Charlie.

**CHILD.** *(sarcastic)* Good one, Becca.

I've never heard that one before.

**BECCA.** What's my name?

**CHILD.** Becca.

**BECCA.** Say it again.

**CHILD.** Becca.

**BECCA.** We can do that.

Together.

We can get close to a hawk.

I like it here.

I like Iowa.

*[MUSIC NO. 13: "I AM A HAWK"]*

**CHILD.**

    I AM A HAWK
    ON TOP OF A TREE HOUSE
    AND I'M TAKING OFF
    I'M IN THE AIR NOW
    I'M ABOVE TREES
    I CAN'T SEE PEOPLE ANYMORE

**COMPANY.**

    OH

**CHILD.**

    I'M GETTING HIGHER

| **CHILD.** | **COMPANY.** |
|---|---|
| I'M GETTING HIGHER | OH... |
| I'M IN THE CLOUDS | HEAVEN AND EARTH DO |
| NOW | NOT TOUCH ONE |
| | ANOTHER BUT OH LOOK |
| | AT THE CLOUDS LOOK |
| THE HIGHEST CLOUDS | THE HIGHEST CLOUDS |
| NOW | |

**COMPANY.**

    HEAVEN AND EARTH DO NOT TOUCH ONE ANOTHER
    BUT OH LOOK AT THE CLOUDS
    LOOK THE HIGHEST CLOUDS

| **CHILD.** | **COMPANY.** |
|---|---|
| I'M IN THE CLOUDS NOW | CLOUDS |
| | HEAVEN AND EARTH DO |
| | NOT TOUCH ONE |
| THE ONES YOU CAN'T SEE | ANOTHER BUT OH LOOK |
| | AT THE CLOUDS LOOK |
| FROM THE GROUND | THE HIGHEST CLOUDS |
| FORGET ABOUT | |
| THE GROUND! | HEAVEN AND EARTH DO |
| | NOT TOUCH ONE |
| | ANOTHER BUT OH |
| FOR SEE | LOOK AT THE CLOUDS |
| FROM THE GROUND | LOOK THE HIGHEST |
| | CLOUDS |

FORGET ABOUT
THE GROUND!

                              HEAVEN AND EARTH DO
                              NOT TOUCH ONE
                              ANOTHER BUT OH
FORGET ABOUT THE              I
GROUND
I'M HIGHER THAN THE           CAN
CLOUDS NOW                    SEE .
                              OH
                              SOMETHING
                              UP ABOVE THE RED SKY!
                              OH
                              RED SKY, OH, OH
STILL GOING UP!               OH...
STILL GOING UP!               ...
STILL GOING UP!               ...

**COMPANY.**

SOMETHING'S BROKEN THROUGH ABOVE THE HIGHEST
  CLOUDS AND
OH LOOK AT IT NOW LOOK OH WOW OH WOW
LITTLE THING CAN MAKE IT ALL THE WAY TO MARS, HA,
LOOK AT IT GO. LOOK, IT'S OUT THERE
SOMETHING'S BROKEN THROUGH ABOVE THE HIGHEST
  CLOUDS, AND OH

**BECCA, CHILD, NANCY DREW..**  **LIZ, AMANDA, CHEERLEADER.**
HEAVEN AND EARTH DO             LOOK AT IT NOW, LOOK,
  NOT
TOUCH ONE ANOTHER               OH, WOW,
BUT OH                          OH

| **BECCA, CHILD,** | **SANDY, ROGER,** | **LIZ, AMANDA.** |
| **NANCY DREW.** | **CHEERLEADER.** | |
| LOOK AT THE | LITTLE THING | WOW |
| CLOUDS | COULD | |
| LOOK THE | MAKE IT ALL THE | |
| HIGHEST CLOUDS | WAY TO MARS, HA | SOMETHING'S |
| | LOOK AT IT GO | BROKEN |
| | | THROUGH |
| | | ABOVE THE |
| | LOOK, IT'S OUT | |

THERE

HIGHEST CLOUDS
AND OH,

HEAVEN AND
EARTH DO NOT
TOUCH ONE
ANOTHER

NOW

LOOK AT IT NOW,
LOOK
OH, WOW, OH,

BUT OH LOOK AT
THE CLOUDS
LOOK THE
HIGHEST
CLOUDS

LITTLE THING
COULD
MAKE IT ALL THE
WAY TO MARS, HA
LOOK AT IT GO

WOW

LOOK IT'S OUT
THERE

SOMETHING'S BRO-
KEN THROUGH
ABOVE THE
HIGHEST CLOUDS

HEAVEN AND
EARTH DO NOT
TOUCH ONE
ANOTHER

NOW

AND OH, LOOK AT
IT NOW,
LOOK, OH, WOW,
OH

BUT OH LOOK AT
THE
CLOUDS LOOK
THE HIGHEST
CLOUDS

LITTLE THING
COULD
MAKE IT ALL THE
WAY TO MARS, HA
LOOK AT IT GO

WOW

SOMETHING'S BRO-
KEN THROUGH
ABOVE THE
HIGHEST CLOUDS

LOOK, IT'S OUT
THERE

HEAVEN AND
EARTH DO NOT
TOUCH ONE
ANOTHER
BUT OH
**COMPANY.**
WOW
WOW
WOW

NOW

AND OH, LOOK AT
IT NOW,
LOOK, OH,

WOW, OH

**End of Play**